For my won
To every member I'm grateful to
have spent time with,
and the generations that came before.

Thank you for your parts in my story.

BLEED

EMERALD
O'BRIEN

PROLOGUE

The misty cloud of her breath rose in the frost—the last of his daughter—evaporating into the dark night as she released her grip on his bloody hand.

He didn't let go. He'd promised to never let go. Only moments before, he'd shouted it at the top of his lungs, from the bottom of his heart.

Tears slipped into the wrinkled paths at the corners of his eyes and down his cheeks, before falling onto her face. He pressed his forehead against hers and sent a desperate cry of anguish echoing through the clearing. Wind shook the yellow leaves on the branches of the oak trees above, and they whirled through the damp air, settling onto the wet grass surrounding them.

He lifted his head, torturing himself with his reflection in her lifeless eyes. A few strands of her hair blew across her face, obstructing his view. As he brushed it away, blood from his fingertips painted two streaks across her forehead. His gaze remained there, transfixed on the blood—her blood. The knuckles on his other hand were white with his grip on hers.

For all he knew, their final moments together lasted minutes, or it could have been hours before the blue and red flashed across her face.

As police officers and paramedics slid down the small hill, emerging from the trees into the clearing, he opened his mouth to call for them. He wanted to call for help, for her, but he knew it was too late. Just as he'd felt the energy of his daughter's spirit when she was brought into the world by his late wife, he'd felt it leave.

Later, he'd look back and wonder if that's when the deep, hopeless abyss began to consume him. He'd blacked out, unable to remember most of what happened down that hill after his daughter's last breath. The terrifying reality couldn't wrap its cold fingers around him in an isolating grip as he closed his mouth and stared back down at his daughter. It couldn't even touch him.

His body shook with rage.

A paramedic dropped to her knees on the other side of his daughter's body as he glanced around them, squinting into the field of darkness, unconsciously losing his grip on his daughter's hand.

A single thought crept into the forefront of his mind as he searched in the night, lifted up and away from his daughter's body by an officer. It wasn't a promise—he'd never make a promise again after breaking it to the only person he had left, the only one he loved, his only reason for living. That's what he believed that night, but this all-consuming thought birthed a new truth.

He'd have vengeance before death.

1

Fox Dallener dumped the last of the washroom garbage into the big, green bag and twisted it shut. She yanked it from the bin in her clenched fist and released a deep sigh. The same time last year, she'd been selling sexy, professional photos of herself in a mask to protect her identity. She wore lingerie, swimsuits, and costumes—whatever the Crescent Moon Studios projects required of her. Each shoot earned her more than she'd made in an entire week at H.G.O.R., Haskin's Great Outdoor Rentals. She tried not to let herself think about the monetary discrepancies or compare the effort it took to work both jobs, especially after the studio went under that spring and she stopped selling pictures of herself entirely.

Closing duties, the most frequent time of her shift when the thoughts of regret and despair did cross her mind, had gotten easier since the end of summer when the cottage rush slowly disappeared. She wouldn't have thought about it at all if it hadn't been for the "For Sale" sign posted outside her front window. Thoughts of big paychecks from past photoshoots with Dylan, the handsome photographer at Crescent Moon Studios whom she used to call a friend—and a crush—lingered, aching in her chest. She hobbled past the bathroom stalls and the row of three mirrors and sinks, her long, red hair shining in the fluorescent light in her periphery. Fox hip checked the door, carrying the bags into the dim hallway.

She glanced to the left, expecting to catch a glimpse of one of her co-workers in the dark storefront. Without movement or sound, she turned right toward the back door and the bright red exit sign glowing above it, guiding her way. Light rock still hummed over the speakers—the same songs she'd heard over the entire summer. Behind the closed door to her left, in the main office, Scott or Elisha would be locking the money deposit away in the safe before turning off the music. At the beginning of her shift, she'd volunteered to take garbage duty off Elisha's hands after she announced she had a date that evening. Without the time to go home to shower or change, Fox would have wanted someone else to dump all the trash out so she could remain clean for what sounded like a romantic evening.

Fox pushed her hip against the icy metal door handle and shoved her way outside, a fully loaded industrial-sized trash bag in each hand, knocking against her sides. She swung them out the door first and followed as she kicked the heart-shaped rock into place, ensuring the back door stayed open so she could get back in.

Maroon-and-golden maple leaves tumbled in the wind across the paved, empty back lot a quarter of the size of a soccer field. They danced with smaller, yellow oak leaves from the trees behind the storage warehouse on the other side of the lot. Fox turned left and stepped around a puddle on her way to the dumpster by the corner of the building. A glint of light behind her caught her attention. The moon reflected off the windshield of a seemingly empty brown car, parked on the small side road by the exit to the far right of the warehouse. Fox glanced around for the owner without luck before turning back for the dumpster again. They could have gone around to the front, and if they tried to book a rental, Elisha wouldn't take a chance on being late for her date. Scott, however, would allow them in.

A hot shower, her favourite pajamas, and the pint of ice cream she'd been saving to enjoy with a scary movie before she had to wake up and do the same day all over again in the morning, if she was lucky, called her name. If Kennedy texted that night and asked her in for an early-morning shift, she'd begrudgingly take it as she always had. A single woman without family nearby needed to provide financial security and stability for herself some-how. For Fox, two jobs had covered her needs, but after the studio went under, she couldn't afford her own apartment anymore. Luckily, when her aunt and uncle separated, they offered her their house to stay in while they sorted things out. To them, "sorting things out" meant they couldn't be in the same place, and while they travelled, they needed someone to rent it until they could sell. They said it would take a while before they put it on the market, and with each passing month, Fox had settled further back into the comforts of the home she grew up next door to, and the luxuries it afforded her.

She set one garbage bag on the cement foundation block, leaning it against the dumpster before shoving the lid open and sending it smacking against the brick wall of the shop on her first try. She hoisted the garbage bag in her hand up and over the side of the dumpster, sending it crashing against the trash below. It echoed from the bin, out into the lot.

Another sound echoed from the other side of the bin, around the corner. *A cough?*

She glanced over her shoulder, clenching her fists and stomach muscles.

Is someone there?

Fox took a step back, trying to peer around the side without getting any closer to the potential danger, her chest heaving with the panic of confronting whatever it was on her own.

No one there.

She turned around, and the brown car was gone. Had it been a cough, or was it the engine in the distance?

A crack of light glowed from beneath the exit door, and shadows of tree branches danced across it.

Fox glanced around, quieting her own breath and tuning into her surroundings as she anxiously reached for the second garbage bag, her back vulnerable and exposed. She swung it back and forth, adding some momentum to it as she scanned the visible section of the lot around her.

Releasing a grunt and the bag, it flew above her, crashing against the back of the dumpster lid and into the garbage below. She held her breath, listening for the sound again, but she heard nothing.

She rose to her toes and pulled the bin lid down, slamming it closed with a *whoosh* that blew her red locks away from her face. She spun around, glancing behind her as her boots slapped the pavement on her way back to the door. Cold water splashed against her ankles from the puddle she rushed through. Her heart raced as she reached the door—the closed door. Their special heart-shaped rock doorstopper sat several feet away. Fox spun around, checking her surroundings as her hand connected with the smooth, metal door handle. She tugged at it without any give her way. She pounded the side of her fist against the door above it. Whoever was in the office would hear her—even over the music—they *had to*.

She turned around, pressing her back against the cold metal door, glancing down at the heart-shaped rock. It could have rolled out from between the door and its frame. It had happened a few times before, and they'd had to go around to the front to get back in. But could it have rolled that far away? Someone could've kicked it.

"Hello? Scott?" She pounded her fist against the door behind her, her chest heaving, struggling for each breath as the possibility became a probability in her mind. "Elisha? I'm locked out!"

No sound came from behind the door.

Fox scanned the dark, empty lot.

Was someone out there, messing with her? Had she

heard them the first time she threw out the garbage? Had they used the noise of the second bag banging around in the dumpster to muffle the sounds of the door closing? It was open before she threw out the second bag. If it slammed shut on its own, she would have heard that, wouldn't she?

"Is anybody out here?" She pressed her side into the metal door handle, wishing it would push her back.

Why isn't anyone coming?

She tucked her hair behind her ears, straightened her posture, took a deep breath, and marched toward the right corner of the building. With a clear path to the grassy side of the building closest to the side road with street lights, she picked up her pace. As she turned the corner, she heard a faint, muffled cough from somewhere far behind her. It was the same noise she'd heard earlier, but this time she recognized the sound as someone clearing their throat. There was no mistaking it.

Someone was back there, watching her.

She picked up her pace, jogging toward the front of the building without looking back.

Was it someone trying to break into the warehouse, thinking they'd all gone home already? No, their cars were still in the front lot. That sound—it sounded far away. How close were they? Would they follow her? She wouldn't be able to hear their footsteps with the grass beneath their feet and her heartbeat thudding in her ears. They could reach out to grab her, and she'd have no warning.

She broke into a run until she reached the front

corner of the building, slowing down to round it. In her periphery, a tall, dark figure rounded the corner from the back of the building, their shoulder swiping against it, as they stalked toward her with a determined stride.

2

The large sign above the front door glowed neon red matching the "Closed" sign hanging in the large window beside it. Fox reached for the metal, rectangular door handle. She yanked on it, sure it wouldn't give like the back door hadn't—sure Scott or Elisha had locked it already like they were supposed to. It flew open. She whipped around, quickly closing the door and twisting the lock. Squinting out the window, she took a shaky step back.

"Someone's out there," Fox gasped over her shoulder into the dark storefront, barely able to take her eyes off the large window wall before her, waiting for the figure to emerge and approach the door. "They were out back, and they took the rock out from between the door— They locked me out—"

"Hey, hey," Scott's low, smooth tone called. She turned as he strode past the racks of outdoor merchandise lining the shopfront, Elisha following close behind. "What's going on? Is someone giving you a hard time?"

"Someone locked me out, and then they—" Fox squinted at the place where the wall met the glass window and pointed to it, waiting for movement. "They followed me to the front."

"Who did?" Scott raised his voice as he joined her side, the shoulder of his matching black company T-shirt reading "Haskin's Great Outdoor Rentals" pressed against her own.

Elisha stepped up on the other side of her, resting her hand on Fox's arm. "Are you okay?"

"Yeah, I'm okay, I just..." Fox nodded to Elisha and turned to Scott. His thick, furrowed eyebrows continued to search the lot. "I don't know who it was. I took the trash out, and I heard someone out there clearing their throat. There was a brown car parked on the side road by the exit, and then it wasn't there the next time I looked, but the rock wasn't in the door, and I was banging on it. Didn't you guys hear me?"

Scott frowned and shook his head. From the corner of Fox's eye, Elisha's chin-length brown hair shook from side to side.

Fox licked her lips and took a step closer to the door. "I came around the side, and when I turned the corner to the front, I saw them following me."

Elisha took a step past her and reached for the front lock, twisting it with no give. Better to be sure. Fox nodded a thanks for the extra precaution.

Scott pressed the side of his temple against the glass, squinting in the direction she pointed to. "What did they look like? Was it a guy or a girl?"

Fox sighed, finally catching her breath. "I didn't

really see them, but maybe a guy. It's so dark back there. Out here in the front lot, there's some lights, but I can't—"

"I don't see anything—" Scott started.

Two beams shone from behind the trees along the main road ahead.

"That car?" Elisha asked, her long, manicured nail tapping against the glass as she pointed to the brown car before it pulled into the front lot.

Fox nodded, stepping right up to the door beside Scott.

"That's my ride." Elisha's cheerful tone added a stark contrast to the panic that remained stationed in Fox's chest.

"Who's that?" Fox asked. "Your date? That was your boyfriend in the brown car?"

Fox turned to face her, stepping away from the door. This guy was just hanging around the back and decided to, what? Chase her for fun while he waited for Elisha?

Elisha shook her head, but she couldn't hide her grin. "Not my boyfriend. It's not serious or anything."

Fox continued to stare at her with concern. Elisha's smile faded as she looked back and forth between Scott and Fox.

"Oh, no, he wouldn't have been following you." She fussed with her hoop earring. "I'm sure it wasn't him."

The brown car sat parked in the last space in the lot to the right of the aisle, closest to the road. How could Elisha be so sure—and so eager to brush her concerns aside?

"What does your boyfriend look like?" Scott folded his arms over his chest, squinting out at the car.

"He's handsome, with short brown hair," Elisha's playful tone almost sang. "A little older, taller than me..."

Elisha stood half a foot taller than Fox.

"He *was* tall, but I didn't get a good look at him, like I said. The streetlights from the side road are too far off. He was in the shadows from the trees." Fox fidgeted with the medallion on her necklace, her fingers gliding along the loop of her father's ring. "There aren't any other cars out there, so... How long have you been dating? Is he the kind of guy who'd..."

"Who'd follow a girl around the back of a building and scare her?" Elisha laughed. Scott turned to her, his eyebrow raised. "No way. We've been seeing each other for a few months now."

Elisha took a step backward, a grin still plastered across her face, and pointed to the back of the shop. "I'm just going to grab my stuff."

She turned and rushed past the merch displays in the small shop lined with hats, helmets, air fresheners, and fishing gear, disappearing down the dark hallway. Scott followed the same path down the middle aisle, rounding the counter.

Fox glanced back to look out the window and scanned the front. She hadn't been attacked, but someone was following her, and who knew what they'd have done if they'd caught up to her? *Why aren't they taking me seriously?*

"You still think he's out there?" Scott called, his

smooth voice back to the natural, calm tone it rarely gravitated from. "Should we call security *now*?"

"There aren't any other cars around..." Fox muttered, letting her arms fall to her sides as she turned toward the back of the store.

Scott stared down at the single computer screen on the counter, his short facial hair casting a dark shade across his jawline by the cool light. "No one's scheduled for a drop-off, and even if someone was trying to return something—"

"There were no cars out there, besides the brown one. Only yours out front." She walked toward him, grateful he was looking into it on her behalf. "I called out and no one answered. If they rent from us, they know the drill. They have to come in the shop—"

"Do you think you might have seen a shadow and thought it was *someone* instead of *something*?" Scott rested his hands on his hips and shrugged.

"A shadow from what? A tree branch?" She shook her head. "Someone was out there. I heard them. I saw them..."

Elisha emerged from the dark hallway with their bags and coats in hand, resting them on the end of the counter where Scott and Fox approached. She'd changed into a cocktail dress and a fresh pink gloss shined on her lips as she grinned, casting a glance toward the front window. Fox had taken the garbage duty for her, and all she could do was rush to leave Fox in her time of need.

"Hey, let's finish up here." Scott tapped the counter, nodding to Fox. "And then security'll be here in no time, and we'll ask them to check around."

Chances were good they'd take her concerns more seriously than Scott and Elisha had—unless it happened to be Ryan's shift. She could only imagine the teasing that would ensue when he realized she wasn't sure what she'd seen.

Fox pulled her vegan leather coat on as Scott returned to the computer. With a few clicks of the mouse, the screen went dark, and the room even darker, lit only by the red glow of the signs out front. Scott hung his flannel coat over his arm. Elisha pulled on her peacoat and grabbed her purse, retrieving her cell phone before hanging it over her shoulder. The screen illuminated her face, glossy lips, and pink cheeks. Fox took out her own cell phone as Scott fished around in the drawer for the keys.

Two unread texts from her aunt awaited her. Fox hovered her finger over the screen.

What if they needed her out by tomorrow? They wouldn't ask that of her without giving her another option until she found her own place to rent. Even if she had another month before they closed on the house, it didn't feel like enough time to find something new and affordable. Not with the rent prices jacked up the way they were.

She took a deep breath and tapped the text message.

Aunt Loralee: *We signed the deal and the paperwork is done. Finally! I'm just leaving now. I'll send you the details tomorrow morning.*

Aunt Loralee: *Don't worry, honey. I know you'll find a great place in no time. Your uncle left you some pizza in the* *fridge and I left you a bottle of your favourite wine in the cellar. Have a good night! Talk tomorrow!*

Dread and distant longing hung heavy in her lungs as she tried to take a deep breath.

A few taps against the front window made her jump, her focus going to the door and the emptiness before it for as far as they could see into the lot.

She frowned, then turned to Elisha. Scott rounded the counter, staring at the front door as Elisha typed away on her phone, oblivious to the noise.

"You heard that, too?" Fox asked.

Scott nodded, the back of his head unmoving, staring at the door.

Elisha set her phone down as Fox walked toward him, then past him, and down the middle aisle, scanning the dark window wall for movement. Banging came from somewhere in front of her, but no one stood before the well-lit front door.

The headlights from the brown car flickered on, shining against another vehicle in the opposite aisle as another bang came from the front window. Fox turned her attention to the banging, and the figure jumped in front of the window into view from the side—the same side she'd run from—smiling.

3

Fox's cousin tapped her fingertips against the glass playfully. She pointed at Fox and released a muffled laugh.

"Jack!" Fox called, relief filling her voice at the sight of her best friend.

Was Jack the one following me, or are they still out there?

Fox rushed to the front door as footsteps followed. She had to get her inside, where they were safe.

"What are you doing here?" Excitement bloomed in Fox's tone, as if her volume could permeate the glass—and maybe it had. She met Jack at the front door and twisted the lock, swinging it open as her cousin rushed into her arms, pulling her close. "Was that you out there? You scared me!"

"I'm sorry." Jack's naturally raspy voice barely escaped from Fox's shoulder. She pulled away with a big grin. "But that *was* kinda the point. I wanted to surprise you."

"What—what are you doing here?" Fox took a step back, taking in the sight of her.

They shared a similar button nose with a thin, slightly upturned tip, and full lips, just like Fox's father and Jack's mother, who were siblings. That was where their common features diverged. Jack's big, warm, brown eyes lit up as she tilted her head down to smirk at Fox from beneath her naturally thick, full eyebrows. She'd tied her coarse brown hair back in a bun, her wavy, wispy front pieces hanging by the sides of her oval-shaped face.

Jack's peachy lips pressed together before she wiggled her brows and shook her head. "You think I'd miss Halloween with you? Not a chance."

"Hey, Jack!" Elisha called to her before turning her attention back to her cell phone screen.

"Hey. Nice dress." Jack nodded to Elisha and Scott, quickly turning her attention back to Fox as Scott nodded back. "I really surprised you, didn't I? You should've seen the look on your face."

Scott shuffled backward and leaned against the counter next to Elisha.

"I can't believe you're here." Fox sighed, finally allowing herself to smile. "I didn't think I'd see you until winter break."

"Ugh, don't remind me." Jack glanced back out into the lot, tugging the sides of her black blazer closed across the front of her black, crew-neck shirt. Her matching medallion necklace hung a little lower than Fox's over the collar, her keychain looped between her fingers. "Almost ready to go?"

Jack shook the keys to Fox's dad's old truck and did

an impatient little dance, swinging her narrow hips from side to side. Scott watched, seemingly fixated on her until he noticed Fox watching him. He turned away, pressing his lips together to hide his smile.

It would be the first Christmas after the finalization of Jack's parents' divorce. They'd speculated on how their family would approach the situation, but no matter what they came up with, they couldn't see there being a positive outcome. The whole family wouldn't be together—hadn't come together since two Christmases before. Jack's parents couldn't hide the tension between them, and instead of trying, they preferred to travel and visit home separately.

Fox returned to the counter and grabbed her bag. "I just got a text from your mom. She said they closed the deal and she'd tell me the details in the morning. Oh, you'll have just missed them. Your dad left this afternoon and your mom just left about an hour ago, I guess."

"That was the point of me coming so late," Jack muttered as Fox returned to her side. "I'll take it as a win that I missed them."

Elisha approached, clutching her cell phone in both hands. "Do you guys mind if I leave? I don't want to keep him waiting too long. Jacob got us a reservation at a fancy restaurant in Toronto."

"No, that's fine," Scott called from behind the counter, sliding the drawer closed. "We'll close up."

Elisha pushed the door open and waved goodbye to them. Fox stepped forward, scanning the front lot again as the door closed behind Elisha. She hustled down the aisle of the lot toward the brown car. If the person following Fox hadn't been Elisha's date, he could still be out there. Elisha reached the car, rounding the front. Fox could barely make out her smile as she opened the passenger side door. The interior light turned on, and a man with facial hair a bit like Scott's turned away from them to face her. His short, brown crew cut looked fresh. He wore either a suit coat or sports jacket with a white shirt underneath it, but from that distance, she couldn't tell much more. There was something about him that seemed older, like Elisha had said. If he'd been the one to follow her, she'd have noticed his white shirt, even in the shadows.

Elisha slid into the passenger's seat and closed the door, enshrouding them in darkness. Fox opened her mouth to ask Jack and Scott if they'd gotten a better look at Elisha's date, but Scott was staring at Jack.

Fox scanned the lot again, watching for moving shadows and listening for any indication they weren't alone. Satisfied—or rather unsatisfied—she turned to Jack. "How long have you been here?"

Jack's eyes twitched in confusion, but she smiled. "You just saw me. I just got here, why?"

"Were you out back at all? Did you see me out there, taking out the garbage?"

"I was by the side there, tapping on the window so you couldn't see me, but I wasn't out back." Jack shook her head, then turned to Scott as he approached with the keys between his fingers. "Why?"

She wasn't the one who had followed her. Fox had known it—the figure had seemed taller than her, and

Jack was an inch shorter—but she hadn't wanted it to be true.

Fox scanned the lot once more, stopping by the front-left corner of the building. "Swear you're not pranking me?"

Scott stopped behind her. "Fox thought she saw someone out there when she took out the trash."

She turned to Jack and sighed. "I got locked out the back, and when I came around the building, *I swear*, someone was following me."

"Ugh, you think it was some perv?" Jack frowned and turned back toward the front door as the brown car pulled out onto the road and a white car waited with its right lights blinking.

"Security's here." Scott stopped at the front door between them. "We'll ask them to look around, okay?" He turned to Fox, his eyes seeming to search hers, waiting for an answer. When she didn't, he tilted his head to the side. "Ready to go?"

Fox nodded with trepidation. Scott pulled the door open for them, and Fox stepped out of the way, walking outside with Jack close behind. Scott turned to the door, his keys jingling. The white security car pulled up along the curb in front of them.

Luke stepped out as Scott handed Fox the keys and Jack stepped toward the curb. Fox tucked them into her bag, remaining between the empty car and the door.

"How's it going?" Luke called, his broad shoulders pushed back as he approached with perfect posture. He scanned them as if to assess what type of night it had been, looking professional as always with his crisp, white dress shirt tucked into his black cargo pants. "You folks having a good night?"

"It's been a weird one." Scott remained by Fox's side, turning to her.

"How's that?" Luke raised his brow, turning to Fox.

She licked her lips, preparing herself to tell the story again in the most credible way possible. She wanted him to believe her—to take it more seriously than Elisha, and even Scott. At least Ryan wasn't working the shift.

"I took the trash out back and put the rock in the door to hold it open, and I heard someone back there. The door closed over somehow, and I couldn't get back in. I came around that side, and when I turned the corner, I saw someone in the shadows following me." *Hunting me. That's what it felt like.* "I didn't see anyone again after that. Elisha had someone come pick her up. His brown car was parked on that side street, but I didn't see him *in* the car. Then, the car was gone. A few minutes later, he pulled into the front lot to pick up Elisha. Then, my cousin came to surprise me."

"Jack, right?" Luke pulled something black from the side pocket of his cargo pants uniform, his titanium wedding band tinted red by the light of the shop's sign above.

"Yeah, hey." Jack nodded, her smile a little wider than it had been all night, her gaze a little friendlier.

"I remember you from the last time we hung out at your parents' place. Man, what was that? Like a year ago, right?" Luke twisted the top of the black cylinder, shining his flashlight in the direction of the side of the building. "I saw that brown car leaving. You didn't happen to get a good look at them?"

Fox squinted in that direction as he began to walk toward the corner. "No. I didn't see much."

It couldn't have been more than a second or two before she ran from them.

"Nobody else saw anything?" Luke called, looking back at them.

Scott and Jack shook their heads.

"I'm going to go around back and have a look. You all stay put until I come back." He ambled toward the side of the building, shining his flashlight along the cement, then off onto the grass.

Fox turned to Jack, feeling the warmth of her presence, her muscles relaxing.

"You want to watch scary movies when we go back home?" Jack asked with a little laugh. "Or have you had your fill of scares tonight already?"

Fox pushed her shoulder with a smile. "It's not funny! Someone could have been waiting back there to attack me!"

"Well, you had Scott here to protect you." Jack nodded to him before turning back to Fox. "And now, you have me."

With Jack, her tension melted away faster. It was just a fact, and it was one of the things she loved most about spending time with her cousin.

Fox turned to Scott. "I guess I don't need a ride anymore. Thanks, though."

Scott nodded to her before stealing another glance at Jack. "Okay, cool."

It was as if he couldn't help but be drawn to her, and to be fair, it was a normal reaction. Jack's soft, delicate features, the tinge of auburn in her brown hair, the hints of freckles on her nose and cheeks, and the beauty mark below her lip all stood out as unique markers on her face, but it was her aura, her charisma, that captured the attention of men and women in her vicinity. Her natural, sultry gaze must have felt something like magic for those attracted to her.

Fox gave him a warm, knowing smile, shoving her hand into her jeans pocket. "You wanna come watch movies with us?"

His eyes opened wider for a second, and even as he tried to suppress a smile, he turned to Jack, seeking her approval.

"Yeah, you should!" Jack's raspy voice echoed in the lot.

"I'll text Costa, too." Fox turned to Jack. "He wouldn't want to miss a chance to see you."

"Sweet. Movie night!" Jack stepped off the curb and stopped between the headlights of Luke's car. She raised her brow and pressed her lips together, her melancholy expression startling Fox. "Maybe the last one we'll have together at my parents' place."

"So, what's the deal?" Scott asked. "They're selling?"

Jack nodded, twisting her body from left to right and shifting her weight from one foot to the other, waiting impatiently. "Sold it officially today, I guess."

"Wow." Scott nodded, pursing his lips in consideration, then turned to Fox. "What will you... I guess you'll be moving?"

Fox nodded and stared into the darkness by the corner of the building that Luke disappeared around. She hadn't mentioned the sale to anyone—friends or co-workers—besides Jack. It was personal, family business, and it hadn't felt real. There never seemed to be a point in telling anyone until it was official. She'd planned on asking if anyone at work knew of a cheap place to rent in Auburn Hills after the house sold, but she'd hoped it wouldn't be so soon. She wasn't financially ready.

Maybe the gig selling sexy pics wouldn't be as hard to do on her own as she'd imagined. It wasn't an issue of difficulty, though. Not really. It just hadn't felt necessary anymore when she moved into her aunt and uncle's.

A beam of light shone along the grass on the other side of the building, catching Jack's eye. They turned as Luke rounded the corner, shaking his head at them.

"I guess he didn't find anything." Jack took a few steps forward toward the middle aisle of the parking lot, so antsy to get on the road that Fox's skin crawled for her.

As Luke approached, clicking off his flashlight, Fox prepared herself for the suggestion that she was seeing things, like Scott had insinuated.

Luke stopped in front of them with a straight face, his fingers rubbing his smooth, freshly shaved chin. "I didn't see anything, but I'll wait for Ryan to get here, and we'll go around the perimeter. Take a better look around. You guys can head out, though. I'll let Kennedy know if we find anything."

So, Ryan *was* working, and it was just a bit of luck that he'd been late.

"Hey"—Luke lowered his voice—"if there's anyone out there, I'll find them."

The wind whooshed and hissed through the last of the tree leaves, the cool breeze unleashing chills across Fox's exposed skin, down to the covered parts, and meeting at the middle of her back.

She shivered, nodding to him and folding her arms over her chest. "Okay, thanks."

"How's the wife?" Scott asked.

Luke had had a summer wedding a few months prior, to a woman Fox hadn't met. When Luke first announced it, Ryan tried to hide his shock, offended that he hadn't been made the best man. Fox wasn't surprised. Best friends from high school grew apart all the time. Luke and Ryan had attended the same one as Fox and Jack—a full four years before they started grade nine.

"Doing great, man." Luke smiled genuinely, unabashedly, for the first time since he'd arrived. Fox stepped around the car, joining Jack's side. "Still putting up with my shift work."

"Hey, it'll all be worth it when you become an offi-cer." Scott stepped off the curb and started down the lot toward the road, where he always parked whatever car he was working on as a side job. "Have a good one! Ladies, I'll see you at the house?"

Fox nodded and watched as he made his way across the lot.

"You worried someone's still out there?" Jack asked, wrapping her arm through Fox's.

Fox nodded.

"Hey." Luke caught up to them and stepped ahead,

guiding them to their vehicle. "Let's keep an eye out for the guy who picked up Elisha. If he comes back around, you let me know."

He stopped in front of the forest green pickup truck that had been Fox's dad's until he passed. Fox's mom never had a particular affinity or need for it with her life of constant travel. She offered it to Fox instead, like they all knew he'd have wanted anyway. Ironically, her fear of driving had stopped her from getting her license as a teen. As a result of the anxiety that accompanied each trial run of driving the truck, she'd agreed to let Jack use it to go to college, with the understanding that as soon as Fox started driving, she'd take ownership of it again.

Luke walked around the perimeter of the truck and stopped by the bed, standing between the tailgate and two oak trees. "You ladies get home safe, okay?"

"Thanks, Luke," Fox called.

"Will do," Jack said, as they both climbed in and closed their doors.

Fox locked hers and watched Scott get into his car by the corner of the lot. A modicum of relief allowed her to rest her back against the seat. Jack turned the key in the ignition. A rock song blasted through the speakers, the bass shaking the truck.

Fox twisted the knob, turning it down as she shot her cousin a look of surprise. "Really rockin' out, huh?"

"He's hot." Jack smirked, nodding to Luke as he walked back to his car. "Like, *really hot*."

Fox smiled, staring after him as Jack pulled out of the spot and turned toward the road. "I thought he wasn't your type?"

"I don't think I have a type anymore." Jack's jaded tone of voice pulled Fox's focus onto her. "I think a man who takes that much care to look after people, to protect them? That's sexy."

They pulled out onto the road, turning right, and passed Scott with his turn signal flashing in the same direction.

Fox waved to him. "It *is* Luke's job to protect people, but I know what you mean. You can tell he's like that for everyone in his life. Probably more so with his wife. You wish Cooper was more like that?"

Jack ran her tongue along the front of her teeth and twisted the knob on the radio the other way. "I broke up with him."

"You what?" Fox shouted over the music. Had she heard her right? "When?"

"Tonight," Jack said, barely audible above the music.

Fox twisted the knob on the radio the other way, almost all the way down. "You didn't tell me you were going to break up with him."

"It was kind of a spur-of-the-moment thing. I knew I was coming to surprise you so we could spend Halloween together. When I told him I was leaving, he told me he didn't want me to go. He asked if he could come see you, too, and I said no. We got into it, and he was accusing me of being selfish and never considering his needs. Then he threatened me and said if I left, he wouldn't be there when I got back."

Fox craned her neck back, studying the tension in Jack's clearly clenched jaw. "Really?"

Jack nodded once before raising her brows, shifting

her left hand off the wheel, and rolling the window down manually.

"He knows how close we are!" Fox's incredulous tone, louder than she'd anticipated, only accentuated her distaste. "Why would he try to keep you from seeing me without him?"

"He seemed to have the impression he was the most important thing in my life. I couldn't take it. Not the arguing, or his self-importance." She licked her lips and pressed her tongue against her cheek, pushing it out as she sighed. "And I don't need an 'I told you so,' okay?"

Fox held her hands up and shrugged before rolling down her own window. Scott's headlights shone from behind them, reflecting off her side mirror, and she knew he'd be thrilled once he found out Jack was single again—not that he'd ever tried to make a move. She was pretty sure Jack had no interest in Scott, and that he probably didn't even have a chance. It wouldn't work anyway because of the distance, but it hadn't stopped Fox from inviting him along for the sole purpose of making his night a little better. Without him, Elisha would have brushed off Fox's concerns, and possibly even left her alone. Yes, if Scott was happy to come along, and Costa would join them, they'd get a fun night together where they wouldn't have to talk about Jack's parents' divorce or the sale of the house. Jack wouldn't have the opportunity to try to convince her to move to be closer to her, or to convince her not to sell any more photos of her body for the money to live independently. After what Jack had confessed about Cooper, they both needed a night to relax and forget their troubles—at least the ones they couldn't control.

"Hey, Jack?" Fox turned to her. "I'm happy if you're happy, okay?"

Jack nodded with a small smile and turned the radio up again. "Let's have some fun this weekend!"

The soothing wind whipped through Fox's hair, simultaneously calming and exhilarating her. They belted out the lyrics to the rock song on the radio, playing on the station Fox's dad had left it on before he died. It was an unspoken rule that they'd always turn it back to his station before getting out, so when the truck started, they'd hear what he'd be listening to if he were still alive.

It was like they were transported back in time, driving off to their next adventure with him. She was with her favourite person in the whole world, with a full weekend ahead of them, and nothing else mattered.

4

He'd seen the circle made of chairs in movies and TV shows—the anonymous facing one another to confess their secrets and sins, one by one. He assumed his first experience in the grief support group would mirror something like those scenes when he forced himself to his first meeting. After voluntarily checking himself into the mental health facility and receiving a blue, hospital-style bracelet, he'd wondered if his attendance in group therapy could somehow lead the way to a life worth living. His wife had given him purpose and happiness before her death, and his daughter had done the same after his wife passed, until her own death.

That night, on the cold, damp grass, after being dragged from her lifeless body, he wasn't sure he'd ever find the will again. It was only on a whim that he'd decided to try to live, and when the energy infused his veins, he got in his car and drove himself to Auburn Hills Centre for Mental Health Sciences, filled out the paperwork to check himself in, and began the program.

But it hadn't led the way to much of anything, except an existence filled with constant pain. No one had forced him to go to group therapy, or to come out of his room apart from eating his regularly scheduled meals and taking his medication. Every day that passed, life seemed even less worth living, and as a group member droned on about the loss of their husband, he stared down at his hands, remembering his daughter's warm blood coating them. The blood on her face.

He twisted at his blue wristband. The pungent, copper odour returned in his memory, and then to his tongue, as if she were right there in his hands again.

"Thank you for sharing, Hayden." The therapist gave her a gentle nod. "I'm sure so many of us could see ourselves in Hayden's story. Would anyone else like to share today?"

He couldn't see himself in her story. He didn't imagine anyone in the circle had felt a pain that could even be compared to his own. No one had spoken about losing a child, and if there was anyone who had, it was unlikely they'd watched them die in a pool of their own blood. No, he couldn't relate to Hayden's story, or her feelings, or her eagerness to share.

The only story that mattered was his daughter's, and late at night, curled up in bed, he knew that she was the only real reason he remained alive. He was the only one left to tell it, and it deserved to be told. She deserved to have been known, and to grow up, and get married, and live the life she chose, and know that her father was in her corner, no matter what. He'd been robbed, not only of the ability to prove that to her, but to provide her with safety. He'd failed to protect her when they took her life before his eyes.

His stomach clenched and twisted, imagining her shocked expression of terror when she realized there was nothing he could do to help her—save her.

He stood, his chair squeaking across the floor. As he stomped out of the circle, headed for the door, the therapist leading the group nodded to him, as if giving him the permission to leave that he never asked for.

He marched down the hallway with several closed doors on either side. Light hit the side of his face, and he squinted against the sun pouring in from the glass wall, facing the courtyard in the middle of the facility. Nearly closing his eyes, he stomped past a group of nurses throwing open the doors. A man's cries flooded the hallway, and he turned to the glass.

A man in his white robe lay on the floor, sobbing and screaming. As the first nurse reached him, he held his hands up to shield himself, revealing a yellow bracelet on his wrist—involuntary placement. The second nurse produced a syringe and knelt by his side.

Slowing to a walk and stopping before the solid wall, he took a few steps back and turned to the window of the courtyard. He had to watch. He had to see if the man could evade the needle for long, or if they'd succeed in subduing him.

"He's been here as long as I have," a man's voice came from behind him.

He turned to see a middle-aged man, about his age, wearing faded jeans and a T-shirt with a light jacket over top. After noticing the wrinkles on the man's forehead as he frowned in the direction of the commotion, he decided he was probably a little older. Faded Jeans held a coffee cup before his lips and blew on it. As the cuff of his black coat receded, he recognized the blue plastic bracelet that matched his own. Faded Jeans rested his cup against his thigh without having taken a sip— without having taken his eyes off the scene unfolding in the courtyard.

"How long's that?"

"Too long," Faded Jeans said. "His family put him in here."

He turned his attention back to the window—to the man in the white robe. He flailed his arms through the air as security caught one and held him down. Everyone in the courtyard watched on from their tables and benches, horrified and fascinated expressions focused on the struggle.

"You wanna hear something funny?" Faded Jeans took a sip of his coffee, and his chest heaved with a deep sigh. "There's a certain peace that comes with knowing I can just walk out those front doors any time I want, but sometimes, I don't remember that's an option."

Oddly enough, he felt the same.

He took a step back, taking a seat beside Faded Jeans, and watched as the nurse pushed the needle into the man in the white robe's arm.

"But that," Faded Jeans said, still staring through the glass, "just might be the reminder I needed."

"You leaving?"

Faded Jeans huffed a laugh and shook his head. "It's like Hotel California."

He shook his head. "I don't know what you mean. We can go anytime."

"Can't leave ourselves, can we? Can't escape what we've done—not in here. That's why folks like you and me are here, isn't it?" Faded Jeans took another sip of his coffee, nodding to the matching blue bracelet. "Out there, it's just a matter of time."

Faded Jeans stood, leaving his coffee on the bench, and began walking toward the front reception area.

"Matter of time until what?" he called after him.

Faded Jeans turned around. His Adam's apple bobbed as he shoved his hands in his pockets, hiding his bracelet. "Till we get what we deserve." He turned around and shuffled down the hallway, his voice trailing off with him. "One way or another."

Karma? No, that's not what Faded Jeans meant, and if it was, that's not how he took it. They couldn't escape what they'd done in here, because whether you were put in here or you chose it, you lived. You were kept alive.

As Faded Jeans turned the corner, he realized what he'd really meant.

Out there, it was only a matter of time until we ended our suffering, one way or another.

Out there, he had a choice, unlike the man in the white robe.

There wasn't much left for him anymore—but he wanted the choice.

Maybe it was time to end it all.

5

Jack eased off the gas as they whizzed past matching streetlights on either side of the truck, reflecting off the hood in the darkness. That passenger side had always been hers, but it hadn't felt right after her father's passing until Jack started driving it. Each time they went out together, Fox watched the town, and the people and places in it, from her side—always the same perspective.

Gripping the wheel with both hands, Jack made the wide right onto the quiet crescent they'd grown up on, side by side. Each of the five houses along the curve of the capital D sat on half an acre of land. They passed the first three while Fox looked out over the field of wildflowers and pine trees between their road and the main one until they reached the fourth—Fox's old house. The people who moved in seemed nice—an older couple from Sterling Heights, the neighbouring city. They said they'd been looking for a quieter place to live in their retirement. She'd see them in their yard sometimes, always caring for the garden beds her mom had made.

A banner of crimson red hung across the top of the stark-white "For Sale" sign on the boulevard before the final, two-storey house. A reminder that soon, the only remnants their families would have left were the trees they'd planted in their backyards and the treehouse their parents had built for them in the woods beyond.

Jack turned left, into the four-car driveway of her childhood home. Scott parked on the other side of the road, opposite the house, beside a large pine they'd once used as a hangout spot after high school with a few of their friends that lived on the street.

Fox hopped out of the truck and flung her bag over her shoulder, rounding the hood. She stopped by the front path and nodded to the sign. "How does it feel?"

Jack pushed her door shut. "Like it's been a long time coming, but I guess it makes it all real, too."

Scott met them on the paved walkway leading to the large, wooden front door.

Fox dug her keychain from her bag and stopped at the door, turning to Scott. "I texted Costa and told him he could invite whoever he's talking to at the moment. He's on his way."

"It's Kerry, right? Isn't he dating Kerry?" Scott shoved his hands in his jean pockets.

"Last I checked." Fox laughed and shrugged.

"Probably best you kept it vague." Scott smiled, and she turned back to the door. "I bet they have Halloween marathons on TV. We could check that out, or we could pick one of our favourite horror movies and just stream it."

Fox pushed the door open, and they stepped into the tight foyer.

Jack dropped her purse on the entryway table and stopped before the staircase. "I might sleep with you tonight, if that's okay?"

"Yeah, of course." Fox joined her side. "Could be the last time you get to stay in your old room."

Jack nodded with a melancholy smile, displaying the first bit of sadness she'd shown since her parents announced their split. Fox knew even before then, and even with the tough front Jack always offered about her parents' separation, she'd have a hard time with all the changes in motion. They'd been next-door neighbours ever since they were born. After Fox's dad passed, she spent equal time in both houses until they graduated and her mom sold their house to travel. Fox had been working at H.G.O.R. since high school already, but she'd needed more income to afford her own place once her mom gave her the news. After responding to an ad in the paper about a local modelling gig where the models retained most of the control, and it was almost all virtual, she had an interview at Crescent Moon Studios. The small, secluded building off a concession road between Auburn Hills and Sterling Heights looked abandoned the first time she saw it. Jack drove her for support, and although she had to wait in the truck, Fox had told her exactly what the job entailed when she'd finished the interview with one of the Kinmont brothers, who owned the studio.

Brady Kinmont told her they organized professional photoshoots for specific clients of theirs, willing to pay big money for models who'd pose exactly as directed in precisely what the client wanted them to wear. The models would remain anonymous, wearing special masks covering their eyes and nose at all times while at work. They could decide which jobs to accept and decline, with the knowledge that the more they accepted, the higher the pay for their future shoots would be. Fox debated taking the job on their ride back home. Jack told her she'd support her either way, especially with the contract clause about remaining anonymous. The company was serious about that part, even insisting the models each have their own change rooms and only interact professionally without ever revealing their identities to each other. The ultimate privacy and protection had been described in the contract. With the freedom to decide which jobs she was comfortable with, Fox chose a mask, was assigned a number, and became a contractor.

After just her first pay, she was able to afford first and last month's rent on an apartment close to the centre of town so she could get around better without a vehicle. She used the ride app she had an account with to get to the studio on the outskirts of town for the few shoots she had each month. It wasn't until Crescent Moon Studios unexpectedly went under that Fox moved into her aunt and uncle's house while Jack went away to college.

The clear pattern resulting in her conclusion had already developed by that point.

Everyone left Fox.

Her father passed away. Her mother sold her house and wanted to travel on her own. Her aunt and uncle were separating and neither would remain a resident of the town they'd all planted roots in. Jack left for college. The studio shut down.

Despite the facts, she'd never felt left behind. It wasn't like her father had wanted to die, and her mother had always been a free spirit. She'd at least waited until Fox graduated to live her life as a nomad. Her aunt and uncle weren't happy together anymore, and she knew her aunt had suffered from depression after her brother, Fox's father, passed. She'd never been the same—nothing was. And Jack had always known what she wanted to do when she grew up. She'd always made decisions so confidently, seemingly effortlessly, and film school happened to be her most recent adventure. Just because she'd left without hesitation didn't mean she didn't care if she'd have a place to come back home to—even if she'd said the exact opposite after discovering her parents were selling. Fox knew it in her heart because there was no one she knew better than Jack, and no one she loved more.

They all left for different reasons, and while it hadn't meant they wouldn't miss their hometown and all the memories they created there, they'd found other things worth leaving for. Fox had no good reason to leave the only place she'd ever known. Auburn Hills held more memories than she could ever recall, and it was the only home she'd ever need. For Fox, those roots their family had planted meant more to her than it had to anyone else.

"I'll pop some popcorn. Scott, do you want to grab

some beers and sodas from the garage?" Jack asked. Scott nodded once. "You know where they are, right?"

"He should," Fox called over her shoulder, setting her bag and keys on the kitchen counter by the back window. "He's here like, once a week."

Missing Jack was inevitable when she left for college, but she'd remained busy with two part-time jobs at the time to keep her afloat. She'd made even more friends with her co-workers at Haskin's, and while they'd occasionally meet out for drinks, her aunt and uncle's house had become the official, economical hang-out spot to watch movies, relax in the hot tub, and play pool in the basement until the early-morning hours.

That "Sold" sign out front meant change. Fox could deal with that, as long as she could find an extra job to be able to afford to live independently in Auburn Hills. Picking up a similar modelling gig, or embarking on a venture of her own on one of the apps, was always an option. It felt like a familiar way to save money to buy her own house, or to go to college if she finally decided on a career path like Jack.

Scott disappeared down the hallway to the garage door as Jack joined Fox in the open-concept kitchen and living room.

"I got some chips and dip on my last grocery shop." Fox pulled the dip out of the fridge.

"Ooh, the best." Jack nodded, grabbing the popcorn pack out of the pantry and digging for the two bags of chips on the shelf. "Hey, you know you don't have to wait to decide what you're doing until Mom tells you the official moving day tomorrow, right? I know you're stressing about where you'll live next, but I think it's the perfect opportunity to come stay with me."

It was only a matter of time before she'd brought it up again.

Fox kept her back turned, digging for the ice cream she'd saved in the freezer. "Oh yeah?"

"The stars are aligning," Jack practically sang, bringing the pantry items to the island countertop. "Don't tell me you don't see it. This house isn't an option anymore. Cooper's moving out of my apartment—"

"Yeah, about that." Fox pulled a spoon from the drawer and peeled off the top of her peanut-butter-and-chocolate-brownie ice cream, lowering her voice. "How are you doing?"

"It was overdue, I guess." Jack peeled open a bag of chips, staring at it as she pursed her lips.

Fox dug into her ice cream. "What do you mean?"

Jack's focus remained on the bag of chips. "I should have left a month ago when he called me a 'fucking bitch.'"

"He what?" Fox craned her neck back, joining Jack at the island and setting her ice cream and spoon down.

Jack looked up at her, her cheeks pink as Scott shuffled into the kitchen, his arms full of cans. He set the beer and soda on the island countertop as Fox waited for him to leave before Jack continued. He looked from Jack to Fox and pressed his lips together, seeming to read the room, then grabbed the unopened bag of chips and made his way into the living room. He plopped down in the corner of the large sectional.

"Yeah." Jack took a step toward Fox, stopping beside

her as their arms brushed against each other, and leaned closer to her ear. "I got back from the bar late, and he told me he'd been waiting up for me. I asked him why he hadn't just come out and joined our friends, and he said I should have respected him enough to be home after a few drinks and not come stumbling in like a drunken, sloppy mess."

Fox raised her brows, and Jack tucked her hair behind her ears.

"I *was* drunk, but I wasn't sloppy, and I knew if we kept talking, he'd just judge me more so I went and had a shower. By the time I came to bed, he told me if I cared about him, I wouldn't do that again. I told him he wasn't my dad and I'd stay out as late as I wanted, and he could just deal with it like a normal person. He got up, grabbed his pillow, and stormed past me to the living room couch. That's when he said it, as he was stomping past me, like a child." Jack swallowed hard and shook her head, grabbing one of the beer cans and cracking it open. "He knew where I was. He was invited to come. He just wanted an excuse to throw a fit."

Fox clenched her jaw, shocked to hear Cooper would call her anything other than "babe."

"It hasn't been the same between us since, and if I ever bring it up, he changes the subject or gives me the silent treatment. I haven't been back to the bar but he has, and he doesn't tell me when he's coming home. I don't care but I think he's trying to get back at me and *show me how it feels* instead of just communicating. That's what I meant by 'a long time coming.'" Jack took a sip from her can.

Fox turned over her shoulder; Scott dug into his bag of chips, eagerly shoving a fistful into his mouth.

Fox turned back to Jack and whispered, "No one has a right to speak to you like that. You never told me."

Jack released a big sigh, holding her beer in both hands. "Maybe I was hoping I was so drunk, I'd imagined it. I think I told myself if it ever happened again, I'd leave, but then he didn't say anything else like that, so I thought maybe things would get better. Spoiler alert: they didn't."

Jack took a longer swig of her beer as the front door creaked open.

"Hello!" Kerry's chipper voice echoed down the skinny front hallway, and Fox instantly remembered her.

"Did someone order a pizza?" Costa's gravelly voice came right after, closer. He entered the kitchen, chest first, with a large pizza box in one hand and a neon orange can in the other—one of his favourite energy drinks she'd rarely seen him without. "Jack! To what do we owe the pleasure of your company?"

Jack chuckled and wrapped her arms around him, even with each of his hands occupied. "It's Halloween! What better occasion to party?"

"We've never missed a Halloween together," Fox announced, proudly. "Ever."

She stepped away, and he pushed the pizza box onto the island counter beside the drinks, fussing with his gray, long-sleeved shirt. His curly brown hair shook, the style piled on top of his head in the same way since Fox had first met him at Haskin's when he started roughly two years before.

Two years older than Fox, he'd attended high school in Sterling Heights, left to pursue a future in medicine in Guelph, Ontario, and then returned after his mother's Parkinson's diagnosis. He'd rented the main floor of a house in Auburn Hills for her to be closer to the hospital and for easy accessibility for a future wheelchair. Even after taking on two jobs to pay for them both and save for long-term care for his mother, Costa struggled to make ends meet. It had been that way since Fox met him.

"Hi!" Kerry's cheery tone continued as she pulled Fox in for a hug. Fox jumped, having not seen her approach. "Nice to see you again!"

Kerry's curly brown hair covered Fox's nose and mouth, and she struggled to breathe until Kerry pulled away, beaming.

She smelled like peaches, or maybe it was her peach lipstick shade that suggested that to Fox. So sweet. Maybe too sweet. "Hey Kerry, nice to see you again."

"Hey, man." Costa nodded to Scott on the couch, and he waved back. "Jack, this is Kerry."

"Nice to meet you." Jack nodded to her, rounding the counter toward the sink across the island.

Fox guessed it was an effort to avoid an awkward hug from the stranger stepping toward her. Jack made eye contact with Fox, wide-eyed, likely wondering what made Kerry so comfortable embracing strangers.

Fox suppressed a laugh with her hand and joined Costa at the island, shoulder to shoulder as he opened the pizza box. "Ah. Pepperoni."

Her stomach growled as she remembered the pizza her uncle had left for her in the fridge.

"To be fair, I'd have brought you some vegan pizza if I'd known. Kerry and I were on our way to pick it up when I got your text." Costa pushed her with his arm and smiled, scanning the island counter. "So, you shush about the pepperoni. Looks like you've got enough snacks here. What is it? Scary movie night?"

"Yes, sir!" Scott called from the couch.

"So, funny thing—" Kerry's voice filled the room as she swept some of her curly brown hair over her shoulder. "I *love* horror movies, but they scare me *so bad*, I'm afraid of the dark for like a week after I watch one, waiting for the monster from the movie to jump out and grab me." She grabbed Costa's free arm, pulling him against her. "But, umm, like you said, it's almost Halloween, so why not? You'll protect me, right?"

"Of course, he will." Jack put the bag of popcorn in the microwave and took out two bowls from the cupboard beside the fridge.

The TV flicked on, and Scott raised the remote, selecting the channel guide. "AMC always has a sick marathon on. I want to see what they're playing. Even if we see something we like that's not on now, we'll just find where it's streaming. Cool?"

"Sounds good," Kerry said, rounding the couch and sitting by his feet. "Nice to see you again."

He nodded, but Fox would have bet his focus remained on the screen. She wasn't sure if he'd been comfortable with all the attention he got from her, not to mention the signs she missed that he wasn't interested in being touched by her. Had Costa ever gotten jealous over the physical touching and attention she gave everyone else? If he had, Fox never noticed. Kerry was the fifth girl he'd introduced to the group that year. After she and Jack had gotten close with the first one, and Costa ended things, it had been difficult to put in as much effort with the rest. He never took dating seriously, and he'd always said it was because he didn't have the time to. Fox believed him, but she wondered if all the women knew his intentions.

The popcorn popped and crackled in the microwave. Fox grabbed her pint of ice cream, spoon, and the dip, carrying them precariously to the living room table. She turned to the TV as Scott scrolled through the channels.

Costa plopped down on the adjacent love seat with the window to the backyard behind him and cracked open his energy drink. "Man, I'm exhausted."

"Been working a lot?" Jack called.

Costa swallowed his mouthful. "Yeah, at both jobs, and then there's my mom."

Sounds of popcorn shaking in a bag came before the smell of butter filled the room.

"Oh yeah, I can imagine," Jack called. Fox turned from the counter island to watch her dump the popcorn into a giant bowl. "How's she been?"

Costa scratched at the scruff of his beard and sighed. "She's not getting any better. I'd rather not talk about it. I come hang with you fools to forget my problems. Isn't that why we all come hang?"

Scott grunted in agreement, and Kerry nodded with a sad smile, turning to Costa on her right. Costa might have confided in her about his mom already. Maybe they were more serious than he let on. If so, she was glad he had more support—support like Jack gave her.

Fox exchanged a look with Jack from the other side of the couch in the living room, across the island where Jack stood. A lump of anxiety formed in her throat. Jack must have understood the empathetic, grateful look in her eyes.

Jack brought the bowl of popcorn to the table and wrapped her arm through Fox's. "Fox gets to choose what we watch!"

"Oh hey, look what's on." Costa pointed to the screen.

"What?" Scott asked, scrolling back up and squinting at the screen. "Is that...?"

Fox turned back to the screen.

"... voluntarily checked himself into the Auburn Hills Centre for Mental Health Sciences less than twenty-four hours after the brutal and untimely murder of his daughter, Piper Cornell. As we reported almost one month ago, a witness from the area, out walking his dog, spotted the father and daughter sitting on two folding lawn chairs. They were being held between the field behind a subdivision of townhouses the Cornells resided in and the road on the secluded northeast corner of Palmerston Park. With them was a man the witness described as wearing a mask that looked like this sketch, wielding a knife."

In the top-right corner of the screen, a sketch of the white skull mask appeared as the news anchor continued about the composite they credited to the witness. It almost looked like a normal skull, if it weren't for the missing row of bottom teeth. Fox couldn't imagine the same situation happening to her and her late father. She shuddered at the thought, and her chest ached for Piper and her surviving father, Slate Cornell as their pictures were imposed on the screen.

There was no denying Slate and Piper were related with their matching sharp features, dark hair, and deep brown eyes. Both the Cornell's hair looked so thick and shiny. Fox's red locks had often been compared to her dad's. From the slight wrinkles by the corners of Slate Cornell's mouth and eyes, to the experience she felt in his stare, Fox imagined how her own father would have aged as the anchor continued.

"Although the witness could not specify the type of knife, and it is still currently unknown to the public, the witness watched the man with the skull mask stab the young woman repeatedly with it, in what he believed to be her chest and stomach area. The witness called the police for help, remaining at a safe distance. He watched The Skull Masked Murderer escape after what he described later that night in a statement to our reporter as a 'horror show.'"

He'd gotten away with it, and for all the people in Auburn Hills knew, he was still right there in their town. It struck Fox that despite the fact the figure following her that night had worn all black, blending in with the shadows, the killer's freedom had added to her sense of being followed. If it weren't for The Skull Masked Murderer, maybe she could have brushed off what she saw as innocent or imagined, but the heightened sense of fear hadn't left Auburn Hills since the night Piper Cornell was murdered and her killer escaped.

"That was unbelievable, wasn't it?" Costa whispered, shaking his head. "Nothing like that's ever happened here. Not while I've lived here anyway."

"That mask is..." Scott said in a muffled voice from behind his hand as he shook his head, "creepy."

Kerry inched closer to the end of the footrest position on the L-shaped sofa, away from Scott and closer to Costa. "Could we turn this off?"

Fox didn't want to hear anymore, either, but she couldn't help but keep watching.

"Once again, for viewers just joining us, we are reporting live from Auburn Hills Centre for Mental Health Sciences, where Slate Cornell, sole surviving victim of the gruesome attack on September nineteenth, has just checked out. He was spotted leaving the facility just before noon today—"

The TV screen changed to black for a moment before lighting up with all their streaming service options. Scott clutched the remote in his hand. He must have had enough—or at least realized that Kerry had.

"That's messed up, man," Costa muttered, grabbing a fistful of popcorn. "Ooh, buttery, just how I like it. You guys think he's still here?"

"Not if he's smart." Jack slipped her arm out from Fox's and walked back toward the kitchen. "Anybody need anything else before we start?"

Kerry stood and stepped to the sofa, plunking down beside Costa. Jack returned with her beer in her hand and offered one to Fox, but she shook her head. Jack extended the beer and her offer to Scott.

"Sorry. Driving."

"Right! Okay, more for me." She sat on the opposite end of the sectional and crossed her legs beneath her, patting the spot beside her as she looked up at Fox.

A knock came at the back door.

Fox jumped, turning toward it. "What was that?"

The single window pane of the back door allowed Fox to see the dark patio outside. No movement.

When she turned back, Jack gave her a blank expression, and Costa frowned while simultaneously asking, "What?"

An eerie feeling of déjà vu swept over her as she remembered the figure following her down the side of the shop in the darkness. No one else had seen them. Had no one really heard that sound? Was she imagining things? Had keeping up with the news about the masked killer affected her more than she'd realized?

Fox approached the back door, her muscles tense, recalling the way the figure walked toward her—determined in their stride, but not overly eager. She'd considered Scott's idea that it had been a customer, returning something late on the way home. She couldn't understand why they didn't call out to her if their intentions had been above suspicion.

A light tapping hit the dark window behind where Costa and Kerry sat, just a few feet from the door as her own reflection came into focus.

Kerry cocked her head to the side, toward the window. "That. I heard it!"

"I heard it, too." Jack stood. "Guys, that's so creepy. After what we just watched..." Her voice tapered off.

Fox took a step away from the glass door. Scott stood

from the couch, joining Fox on her left. The sensation of déjà vu returned again as they stared out the window, side by side.

Jack approached from her periphery. Fox squinted through the darkness, considering turning on the back patio light.

"I can't see anything." Fox took a step toward the switch to the right, above the counter.

"Shhh," Costa hissed, like a gentle suggestion for them to listen.

Jack shook her head and stepped past him, joining Fox's right side.

Fox stopped and turned to her. "After what happened at the shop..."

Jack nodded and stepped forward. "I'll go—"

"I'm just gonna check it out," Scott said, beating her to the door handle. "I'm sure it's nothing."

"You're going out there?" Fox craned her neck back, frowning.

Just hours before, he'd remained inside the store after she was sure she'd been chased. She'd never thought of him as the guy needing to prove just how courageous he was. He was the calm, cool, collected one. The one who almost managed to make her feel like maybe she'd been overreacting.

"I don't think you should go," Kerry called from the couch, her voice void of its usual brightness. "I mean, I haven't heard anything else. Maybe it was just the wind?"

"I'll be right back." Scott pushed the handle down and opened the door.

Fox and Jack exchanged a knowing look, wishing he hadn't just said that.

Scott stepped outside, ushering the damp night air on the breeze inside before pulling the handle to close the door behind him. It didn't close all the way, and Fox and Jack shot each other a look, neither of them moving to close it.

"Nah, this is not a good idea." Costa turned his neck toward them, raising his voice as he realized Scott's absence. "Let's just come on back and sit and enjoy a movie!"

Fox inched toward the light switch, the cool wind blowing across her face as she reached for it, squinting through the small crack in the open doorway.

Scott took another few steps, disappearing into the darkness.

6

From the dark backyard, crickets chirped in the distance, off in the woods beyond the well-manicured lawn. Fox reached the light switch, her finger hovering over it as she held her breath. *What if he's out there?*

"What are you doing here?" A male voice carried on the wind.

She froze, turning back to Jack.

She frowned, Jack's panicked expression likely matching her own as she hissed, "Was that Scott?"

"What's he saying?" Costa called from the couch.

Fox summoned her courage and flicked the switch up, illuminating the white rock patio slabs with the covered hot tub to the left and patio furniture to the right—all empty. She pressed her face closer to the crack in the door, listening. Jack did the same on her right.

Costa twisted around on the couch to look out the back window behind him. "Where'd he go?"

Fox scanned the tree line, waiting for a figure to emerge, and reached for the door handle.

"Wait—shit!" Costa shouted, kneeling on the couch cushions with his hands pressed against the glass. He leaned back and turned to them. "He's running!"

Scott emerged from the dark, left corner of the backyard, sprinting across the patio into the pool of light by the back door. Panic filled his eyes.

"He's coming," Scott blurted as he pushed his way inside.

Fox and Jack stumbled back, making room for him as cold air burst into the room, sending chills across her flesh at the words.

"Who's coming?" Kerry asked, squinting out the window in the same direction Costa focused on.

The panic from her own chase that night struck a nerve in Fox; she wouldn't wait to see who it was. She grabbed the handle of the door and pulled it closed after Scott, twisting it locked.

"Who?" Kerry scrambled from the couch and pulled her cell phone from her pocket. "What happened? Should I call the police?"

From the outskirts of the backyard, in the direction Scott had run from, something white swayed back and forth—a masked figure, emerging from the darkness.

"Who?" Kerry repeated, her shrill voice becoming an owl's incessant cries as she tapped Costa's shoulder.

Walking at a steady pace, the figure in black strode across the fresh-cut grass, and as they neared the light, the mask revealed itself. A mask like the sketch from the TV. A skull with the bottom row of teeth missing.

The mask the killer wore. Fox's breath caught in her throat as she grabbed Jack's arm. *He's here.*

"Holy shit!" Costa shouted, scrambling from the sofa and backing up into Kerry. "No way."

A black hood hid the top and sides of the skull mask, but there was no mistaking it. The tall figure crossed the patio at a slow, steady pace and stopped just a foot before the door. All three took a step back as the figure pulled their hand from the front pocket of their hoodie, and waved at them— With a bare, white hand? Fox stared on in shock and confusion.

The masked man cocked his head to the side. *Hello, again.*

Although the eyes of the mask were made of black material, she felt his chilling stare and grasped Jack's arm even tighter, frozen in fear.

The masked figure cocked his head to the other side. *Can I come in, or would you like to come out?*

"Call the police!" Costa shouted from behind them.

Scott reached for the door. "No, wait. Hold on." He pinched the lock between his fingers.

"Scott!" Jack screamed.

At the same time, Fox shouted, "I locked it!"

"That's enough." Scott's cold tone, seemingly detached, shocked her.

He stared at the masked figure and gave his head a slight shake as if to call them off—as if they could hear him. Maybe they could.

The masked figure pulled their other hand out from their pocket, producing a large kitchen knife.

Jack screamed and grabbed Fox's arm, pulling her away toward the island.

"Hey, it's okay. Trust me." Scott looked over his shoulder to her, using the same calm voice, and turned back to the door.

As he twisted the lock open, he pulled the handle down. Fox lunged at him, slipping out of Jack's grasp, grabbing his arm.

Scott pulled the door open with his free hand. "Hey, that's *enough*."

Muffled laughter filled the space between the kitchen and living room where they stood. The masked figure stepped back and pulled his hood off, revealing the entire flexible plastic skull that covered his head. He tucked the knife into the hoodie front pocket and reached up toward the back of his neck. His fingers slipped beneath the thin plastic, pulling the mask off, releasing the familiar laughter—more like cackling, she'd always thought—and revealing a wavy mess of brown, ruffled hair.

"Ryan!" Fox shouted. He tugged the mask over the rest of his face, his hazel eyes twinkling by the kitchen light. "What the hell?"

It wasn't The Skull Masked Murderer and Scott must have known it. A shiver ran down her back as Fox released the tension in her jaw. She folded her hands over her chest.

"*Ryan*?" Costa shouted with a baffled glee, pulling Kerry's arm with her phone in it away from her. "It's our buddy. Are you joking, man? Scott, were you in on that? I can't believe it! You got us."

Costa joined them at the door and clapped his hand

against Scott's back as Fox and Jack stepped back toward the kitchen island together, exchanging a shared look of frustration.

"No way." Ryan shook his head and playfully shoved Costa away from Scott. "Credit where it's due—this was all me. My plan, perfectly executed with the unexpected help of Scott."

Ryan ran his fingers through his once-gelled hair, pushing it back away from his face.

"You really scared me," Kerry called.

Ryan smirked and folded the floppy mask before tucking it into the back pocket of his pants.

"I didn't know he was planning on doing that." Scott sighed as he stepped back closer to the kitchen, between Fox and Ryan. "I caught him out there—"

"He went along with it, like a good friend should." Ryan slapped his hand against Scott's chest as he passed him—the tallest of the group and almost a full head taller than Scott—and grabbed a can of beer from the kitchen island beside Fox. He lingered there beside her. "Speaking of good friends, they don't forget to invite you to hang out."

He cut his gaze down to Fox, acknowledging her for the first time while cracking the beer open. He thought it was just a funny prank. Where had he gotten that mask? Why did he think it was okay to pretend to be a killer still on the loose? He wanted a reaction, but she wouldn't give him any more of hers.

"Must have slipped my mind." She grabbed the beer from Ryan's hand and took a sip before walking back to the living room. "Thanks for opening it for me."

"You really had us there!" Costa laughed, shaking his head beside her. He leaned in toward Fox and lowered his voice. "I'm the one who told him we were getting together. I didn't realize you weren't going to invite him. Sorry."

She shook her head, waved him off, and turned back to Ryan. His face beamed with pride, his dimples deep enough to show beneath the scruff of his short beard and mustache.

"You expect any less from me?" Ryan scoffed and winked at Jack. "You're back!"

Jack walked past him nonchalantly into the living room. "For one weekend, and one weekend only."

She'd probably had the same idea as Fox, not to give him any more attention. Her father had always told them to reward the behaviour of those who deserved it and ignore the behaviour of the people who didn't. They'd never been a fan of Ryan's dark humour, but with a killer still on the loose, his timing and taste were more abhorrent than usual. As the eldest of their group of friends, and the least mature, he was the only one who'd been working at Haskin's Great Outdoor Rentals for longer than Fox. He'd only managed to keep his job because the owner was his father's best friend. Ryan's father owned a security company he'd also been working for since he'd come of age. His father made it part of the deal that his company would patrol Haskin's around closing time and every few hours after to ensure employees were safe after dark and property wasn't stolen.

"This weekend only, huh?" Ryan pulled his knife out and set it on the island counter with a clang. "Well, that's excellent timing, because speaking of invites... unlike *some people*, I'm all-inclusive with mine. You guys have to come to the party on Old Watermill Road. Goldie, a buddy of mine, is throwing an old-fashioned kegger. I already paid for you guys, so you're coming!"

"Is that a real knife?" Kerry asked, walking into the kitchen to check it out.

"I wasn't going to do anything with it. No big deal." Ryan laughed and pulled off his black hoodie, revealing a white T-shirt that read *Your mom is my cardio*. "So. Party. Halloween. What do you guys say?"

"Perfect!" Jack wrapped her arm over Fox's shoulder. Fox wasn't shocked she'd want to attend, but her aggravation grew at the realization Jack hadn't left it up for discussion. "We can shop for costumes tomorrow."

"I work tomorrow—"

"Same." Costa sighed. "Closing with Fox."

"Get Kennedy to do it." Ryan grabbed another can of beer. "She never minds when I dip out early."

Fox bit the side of her cheek instead of reminding him it was because he got preferential treatment, and no one else could get away with that even if they wanted to.

"I'm in!" Kerry dropped back onto her spot on the sofa by the back window and patted the cushion next to it, staring up at Costa. "Can we please go after your shift?"

"What about you? You're in, right?" Ryan joined Scott's side and draped his arm across his shoulders, leading him into the living room.

"I don't know..." Scott rubbed the back of his neck,

nudging Ryan's arm off. "I'm working on Big Ruby, and I'm supposed to get a piece in tomorrow for her..."

"On Halloween?" Jack asked. "Come on, you're not even scheduled to work at Haskin's, and you're fixing up a car you could work on anytime? Guys, I'm not around too often, and I wanna party with you while I'm here."

So much for our last weekend at the house together.

Costa shrugged and turned to Fox. "I gotta check with my mom—see if she needs me—but maybe we could go after we close?"

"Yes!" Kerry's curls bobbed up and down as she bounced on the cushion, grasping Costa's arm and pulling him onto the couch.

"Pleaaase?" Jack pouted, squeezing Fox closer, pressing their sides together as if conjoined at the hip and giving Scott her puppy dog eyes.

Scott bit at his lip and as he released it, he smiled. "Okay. I've actually got a costume idea already."

"Yes!" Ryan pulled out the mask from his pocket with his free hand and waved it in the air. "I've already got mine."

"That is so gross, Ryan." Fox shook her head. She couldn't help but say something. It was worse than poor taste. It was cruel. "The killer hasn't even been caught yet—"

"I don't need a guilt trip from you, Foxy." Ryan studied the mask, his grin remaining. "And these are already sold out in every costume store from here to Sterling Heights. I got the last one on my way over."

"Good for you," Jack said, sarcasm oozing from her tone as she leaned her hand against the side of Fox's.

"What do ya say, Lucy? Chill night in tonight? Party the night away tomorrow?"

It wouldn't be quality time, or at least not what Fox considered quality, but after Jack's break up with Cooper and the trip she made out to surprise her, she couldn't bring herself to disappoint Jack. Besides, if there were ever a party worth going to, which Fox could have argued there wasn't, it was a Halloween party. Plus, the fact that Jack had used one of the childhood nicknames only their families called them tugged on her heartstrings. Fox missed the simpler times and their escapades in the vein of Lucy and Ethel.

"How can I say no to my Ethel?" Fox sighed with a smile.

Jack screeched with excitement, pulling her into a hug.

Ryan and Kerry high-fived, and as Ryan's hand dropped, his face twisted in confusion. "It's... Kerry, right?"

She nodded, her sunny disposition even brighter, as if remembering her name correctly was a feat to be rewarded for. Had they made her feel that way? Fox would make a better effort with her in the future.

"This is going to be *way* better than last year," Costa said, more to Scott than anyone.

"What did you guys do last year?" Scott asked.

"We did this lame work-party thing." Ryan rested against the side of the couch. "All the GM's idea, and at that point, it was Richmond. At least if Kennedy had been running it, we could've controlled the playlist, had some drinks—"

"The worst part was"—Costa lay back on the loveseat, resting his legs on Kerry and taking up all the space he physically could as he stretched—"it was mandatory. We had to give out candy to customers all day, and then they advertised candy for kids until whenever they stopped coming."

Fox had called in at the last minute to cancel her job with Crescent Moon Studios when Richmond, their old manager, made the party a mandatory shift. She'd lost out on the eight-hundred-dollar gig, which all but guaranteed she wouldn't be offered another like it for months. When she finally got home from Haskin's to hang out with Jack, they'd watched horror movies and enjoyed copious amounts of candies and chocolates until they were sick and tired and passed out in sugar comas right there in the living room to one of their favourites —*Halloween.*

Scott started to walk toward the opposite side of the couch, but Jack grabbed his arm, stopping him.

"Hey, that was pretty brave what you did—going out there when you didn't even know it was Ryan. Wanna be my bodyguard and escort me to my truck? Help me bring my bags in?"

"Sure." Scott could barely contain his grin, pressing his lips together as the smile remained in his eyes.

"Bags? Plural?" Ryan asked. "I thought it was *one weekend only?*"

Jack walked into the hallway, ignoring Ryan, and disappeared near the front door.

"Hey," Scott lowered his voice as he leaned in closer to Fox. "Sorry for going along with his shitty prank. After what happened to you tonight... I obviously wasn't thinking—"

At least he'd realized it was insensitive.

"It's fine." Fox gave him a terse smile, and he followed Jack into the hallway.

The front door creaked open as Ryan plunked down on the couch in Scott's corner spot next to the sofa and grabbed the remote. "Hey, you know what's an awesome movie? *As Above, So Below*."

Kerry took the remote from him. "Jack said it's Fox's choice. That *is* a good one. Or how about *Scream*? That's my favourite."

"Sure," Fox muttered, inching as far away from Ryan on the couch as possible as she sat and pulled her legs up beneath her. "Thanks, Kerry."

Costa grabbed a bowl of popcorn and rested it on his stomach. "Hey, man, I thought you were working with Luke tonight?"

"Nah, I called in sick, and then I switched shifts to have the whole weekend off." Ryan pulled the remote away from Kerry.

"Must be nice to be able to just drop shifts like that." Costa shoved a handful of popcorn in his mouth.

"Gonna make a joke about me living in my parents' basement?" Ryan asked, staring at the screen. "How original."

"Not all of us have the luxury of living rent-free," Costa said with a mouthful.

"I pay rent," Fox and Ryan said at the same time.

Costa chuckled, his raspy laugh warming the room. "I was referring to Ryan, but hey, even if you *were* getting a free ride, I see it's almost over. Where are you moving to?"

He must have seen the sign out front.

"Not sure yet," Fox muttered, the words ushering in a heavy weight sinking further into her chest. "Let me know if you see any places for rent in town."

Not knowing where she'd live next or how she'd be able to afford it made her so flustered, she couldn't have said anything else if she'd wanted to.

Jack and Scott shuffled into the front hall, the door creaking closed behind them as they re-entered the house, their muffled laughter echoing in the hallway again.

"You're not leaving us, are ya, Foxy?" Ryan turned to her, but she didn't make eye contact.

She stared at the screen until Jack and Scott returned to the living room. Jack took the remote from Ryan and switched on an old favourite of theirs—*April Fool's Day*—but Fox couldn't lose herself in the story. She knew she didn't have much longer in one of her favourite childhood places—the only safe space she had left—but it was all becoming unavoidable, and final, and there was no room to mourn the life she'd had on Hawkstone Drive with her family.

All that would be left of that life for her in Auburn Hills were their material possessions in a storage locker, her father's grave, and the inconsistent presence that was Jack. Thinking about it made her anxious, desperate to cling to the constants: her job; a similar side-gig to the one she'd had before, selling sexy photos of herself; the co-workers she'd forged friendships with; and the town that had always been her home.

Just because everyone else had decided to uproot their lives didn't mean she had to.

She'd plant herself right where she wanted to grow and become so unshakable that no one would be able to move her.

7

Wind hissed through the leaves of the maple trees to his right as he shoved his gloved hands into his pockets, striding alongside the curb without streetlights. He counted the houses, stopping across from the one before the house with the white sign out front. He glanced around over his shoulder. Some of the windows in the other houses glowed in the darkness. No car engines could be heard, no headlights could be seen, and no one was walking on the same street.

He turned to the house across from him and checked his watch, nodding one, two, three times. He sprang forward, jogging across the road and up the empty driveway toward the side of the dark, grassy alleyway between the homes.

Sprinklers whooshed on behind him, water springing from the clicking mechanism in the middle of the front lawn. They sprayed halfway across the empty driveway, not a drop landing on him.

He was already in the dark crevice between the

houses as he slowed to a walk, double-checking that the windows on the side of the sprinkler house were dark. He pressed himself against the brick wall, never taking his eyes off the house with the white sign.

The lights in the dining room were off, as usual, but a warm light from the living room down the hallway illuminated the table and chairs. The rest of the windows on the side of the house were on the second storey—and dark. He relaxed as he approached the backyard. The smoky smell of burnt leaves lingered in the air. He controlled his breathing as he peered around the corner of the brick wall at his back.

No sign of the neighbour's big bully breed out in their fenced-in yard. Good. He'd be able to cross over past the back tree line without him barking, protecting his property, as he should.

Don't worry, good boy. I'm not a threat to you. You're a loyal boy, protecting the people you love most, guarding them with your life.

He only spent a moment crossing the patio in the pool of bright light from beside the back door. It wasn't usually on at this time, but he wasn't deterred. Someone would have had to be standing by the back windows watching his exact spot to catch him in the seconds he took to cross through the light to the shadows.

He took his place beyond the pines and focused on the people in the glowing kitchen window. They laughed and enjoyed their lives together in the way his daughter used to—in a way she'd never be able to again. Rage pulsed through his veins as he took a step forward, careful to remain in the shadows as he had for so long, watching, waiting for just the right moment.

Maybe entering the psychiatric facility had been one of the few mistakes he'd made since his daughter's death. He'd wanted to see something different, but during his time there, he'd only thought about all of them out here.

He watched as one of them approached the window, drink in hand. They turned off the outside light, allowing him a sharper focus on their smiling faces. Out here, this was all he'd seen—people carrying on with their lives as if nothing was wrong, without a care in the world.

He'd looked for a different way while inside the facility, but in the end, he'd seen enough to know *this* was the only way. He had the control, and they didn't know it. They'd never understand until he showed them.

8

Fox stepped out of the steamy shower, wrapped a towel around her body, and shuffled down the hallway toward her room—well, Jack's room... But for how long? The question had consumed her thoughts since she'd woken, lying paralyzed in bed. She'd finally forced herself to get up and go out for her morning walk while anxiously awaiting her aunt's text that never came. Although Auburn Hills was nowhere near as expensive to live in as the neighbouring city of Sterling Heights—or Toronto—with only one full-time job at just above minimum wage, she wouldn't have the money to pay for rent and living expenses on her own. She needed an extra job, and whether it was selling photos on an app or finding something part-time that could work around her Haskin's hours, she had to do it soon.

Jack had remained fast asleep in her room, eventually taking her shower while Fox was out.

"Happy Halloween!" Jack called from the kitchen downstairs. "Wanna pick up breakfast on the way?"

"Sounds good!" Fox stepped into her room, her stomach already growling since she'd returned that morning. "Happy Halloween!"

Fox fastened her necklace on—the matching one she and Jack each had, with a circular pendant they'd received on their sixteenth birthdays. They weren't completely matching, though, as Fox decided it was the best place to keep her father's engineering ring.

After running a brush through her natural red waves and getting dressed in her jeans and black Haskin's T-shirt, the front door creaked open downstairs.

"Meet you in the truck!" Jack called.

Fox scrambled to grab her phone from the charger beside the bed and stopped before her closed closet doors. If she continued selling sexy photos of herself, she might not find an audience who'd be interested if her face was covered. That thought, along with her black mask resting in the closet, had been constantly lingering in the back of her mind. She wouldn't do it without the mask that protected her identity. She'd agreed to take pictures that strangers had used to fantasize about her in the first place because the protection of her identity had been a top priority. Just a year prior, she'd been willing to risk the possibility of those photos being viewed by someone who *knew* it was her, but now, the ability for someone to make that connection left her feeling so out of control and excruciatingly vulnerable, she pushed the idea of getting back into the business at all out of her mind and bounded downstairs to the kitchen.

She put some leftover pizza from her uncle into a container and threw it into her work bag along with a red apple, digging through it for her keys. She stopped as her fingers glided over her cell phone and pulled it out, tapping the screen. No new messages from her aunt. She went to toss it back into her purse when a chime notification stopped her. Fox checked the photo memory—a selfie she'd sent Jack the morning before her first photoshoot at Crescent Moon Studios.

They'd had an end-of-summer bikini shoot, but instead of pictures by the pool, they'd been taken in the dark studio with two other women about her age. They'd always worn masks with winged edges to cover their eyes and noses, but that first time, they'd been given ones that glowed in the dark. The set had been surrounded by neon flamingos and palm trees glowing from the walls. The props included blow-up water floaties shaped like fruit: a banana, a cherry, and Fox held a watermelon wedge. The pictures were all for the same client, who'd apparently had a thing for bikinis and tropical fruit.

Shoots like that one had been fun, and although the girls were never allowed to speak to each other, they'd always worked well together on group shoots to get the best shots for the assignment. The Kinmont brothers took their cut, of course. After the business suddenly closed down, she never heard from them again. It hadn't quite felt like a relief, but she hadn't been disappointed, either. She'd never been passionate about modelling—it was always a means to an end.

She locked the front door behind her and hopped into the truck, hoisting her bag onto the seat between them. Her father's favourite rock channel radio hosts were talking and making jokes about their best- and worst-dressed colleagues' costumes.

"Breakfast burritos?" Jack asked.

Fox's mouth watered. "Yes, please."

As they approached the cemetery on the way to the fast-food restaurant, they both turned in the direction of James Dallener's gravesite.

"Still going every Sunday?" Jack asked.

"Yeah." Fox slid her finger along the soft wedge where the window rolled up. "I used to stay a while, read a book if the weather was nice, or just talk to him. I'd even bring something he might have liked, but... my heart feels so heavy. It's like the more time that passes, the farther I feel from him, and there's nothing I can do to change it."

Fox turned to Jack, who gave her a sympathetic smile before they stopped behind some cars at the intersection. Fox turned to the old maple tree that marked the spot by her father's grave.

"The time I spend there now... the things I bring, it doesn't make a difference. He's slipped away from me so much already. The memories..."

"Mine are foggy, too, but they always have been. You've always had a better memory than me. The stories we all tell—they keep those memories alive." They pulled forward and stopped before the white crosswalk line as the light turned red again. Jack turned to face her. "I know it's not Sunday, but do you want to go for a visit?"

The tighter she'd tried to hold onto him, the further he felt. The only thing that had changed her perception was when her aunt and uncle announced the house was up for sale. It forced her to realize she'd have to move, and when considering where to relocate, she'd never imagined leaving town. The thought had only ever crossed her mind after Jack had invited her to live together in Kingston, Ontario. When she realized she might not have the same proximity she did to the cemetery, she remembered how lucky she was to still be so close to the gravesite, and their houses, and all their old haunts, and just how much she'd taken them for granted. She could visit her father's grave every day if she'd wanted to, and she hadn't been taking advantage of it. The ability to revisit all the places that held so much meaning to her couldn't be taken away.

Fox sighed and nodded.

It might not make her feel any better, but then again, she held out hope that the next visit would reconnect her to some forgotten memory or feeling that would bring her father's spirit back just a bit stronger and give her just a little more to hold onto.

Jack made the turn into the cemetery, and they parked just before the path to her father's grave beneath a fifteen-foot-tall maple tree—the one they'd had planted when he was buried. It now offered shade and a cool place to just sit and be.

They stopped in front of his headstone and circled it to the front. Jack leaned against the tree.

Fox crouched beside it in the short, lush grass. "Hey, Dad."

"Hey, Uncle J." Jack smiled down at the headstone. "Long time, no talk."

Jack never visited the site without Fox because she believed his spirit was all around them, but she humoured Fox whenever they were together, directing her focus and energy to his grave.

"School's... well, there's some good parts and some not-so-good parts. I was with this guy, but I ended things. I guess you know that. You probably knew he was bad for me all along. Like Fox did." Jack laughed to herself and ran her finger along the bark as she shifted her focus to the tree, muttering in her raspy tone, "I guess I did, too."

"Your sister and Uncle B sold the house." Memories of her dad and his sister gleefully telling new people they met that they'd had the luck of purchasing houses side by side formed a hard lump in Fox's throat, and she cleared it before continuing. "The 'Sold' sign's right there on the lawn."

"End of an era," Jack said in a honeyed tone, then she sighed with a smile. "Wonder what your dad would've thought about the divorce..."

Fox leaned her back against the tree, alleviating some of the pressure of her weight from her knees and ankles. "I guess he'd be sad. He'd just want everybody to be happy, I think."

"I think so, too." Jack pushed herself off of the tree and stood on the path before the headstone. "We're celebrating Halloween together again this year. He'd love that, too."

Her dad had always enjoyed a reason for a party, and while he wasn't very creative with his costumes, her mom always dreamt up something and made it come true.

"Remember the time your mom made them each dress as members of Fleetwood Mac from the *Rumors* album cover?"

Fox grinned. "Yeah, that was one of their best."

Jack reached up toward the remaining leaves of the maple tree and ran her hand through them. "My favourite was when my mom went as Dorothy, my dad as the Scarecrow, your dad as the Cowardly Lion, and your mom was the Tin Man."

Fox nodded. "And remember when she made them each into playing cards? King of hearts for your dad, Queen of hearts for your mom, Joker for my dad, and she was the... What was she again?"

"Hmm... I don't remember." Jack shrugged.

It had been so long since their parents were all together, even without her father, that she couldn't remember which card it was either. Anxiety swelled in her chest. She hadn't seen her mom in almost a year—since Christmas—when she'd come home from traveling and the three of them spent it together because Jack's parents were on separate vacations—unbeknownst to anyone—officially filing for divorce. She missed her mom, but she also felt detached in a different way than she had from her father. Her mom consistently chose to be anywhere else but home—or at least, where Fox considered home.

"It wasn't even a face card, was it? I'm sure she had a good reason, whatever it was. She's so creative with that stuff." Jack glanced at Fox, and as if she could read her, she changed the subject. "What should we go as this year?"

Fox stared at her father's grave and then squinted up at the sun shining through the leaves as they blew in the breeze. The sun shone so warm and bright, but Fox shivered beneath the cool shade of the tree. She folded her arms over her chest and rose to her feet, standing in the pain of all the family changes she'd had no part in creating. She had to leave—to think of something else and get into a better mood so she could appreciate the rest of her time with Jack.

Sorry, Dad. No luck this time. Love you, and I'll see you again soon.

"Fox? You okay?"

Fox shook her head and walked back onto the path. "Let's go browse what the costume shop has left."

Jack nodded and wove her arm through Fox's. They left down the path they'd come on without looking back.

9

Fox popped the last of her breakfast burrito into her mouth and balled the wrapper up before chucking it into the garbage bin on their way into the costume store. They searched the first pilfered aisle for something that intrigued them, but neither produced anything for the other.

"*You* like Michael?" a guy asked from the next aisle.

The girl from the group standing in the aisle, seemingly just a few years older, nodded as they passed them. She looked up at Fox as she walked by, no recognition in her eyes. Lynda had babysat Jack and Fox when they were younger, but they hadn't seen her for years after she moved away from Auburn Hills.

Lynda turned back to the guy who spoke. "Yeah. *Halloween* is my favourite horror movie."

"Oh," Jack called, racing to the end of the aisle. She grabbed a bright-red-and-orange pom pom, tossing it to Fox. "What about these?"

"Cheerleaders?" Fox put it back on its hook as Jack grabbed the green ones.

"No. *Dead* cheerleaders!" She shook the pom pom in Fox's face until she laughed and pushed it away. "Okay, fine, not cheerleaders. We could be a dead version of something, though, right?"

"If you want... Hey did you recognize Lynda back there?"

"Where? Our old babysitter, Lynda?" Jack peered around her and shrugged.

"Want to go say hello?"

"Listen, what I want is to cheer you up and get you in the Halloween spirit." She shook her green pom poms. "Puns intended."

"It would cheer me up if I knew we were just watching scary movies at home." The lingering anxiety from the last word kept her from checking her phone in her bag for the dreaded text. "Remember when Lynda would watch us, and we'd watch scary movies with her?"

"Yeah, she's the one who got us into them. But, Fox, we did that last night. Come *on*. I think you need to get out and have some fun... and I think I know what we should go as..." Her grin spread as she brushed a loose piece of wavy brown hair from her face. "And we already have most of what we need for it!"

"What's your idea?" Fox smiled, recognizing the same look her mom used to get when she'd decided on costumes for their parents.

Jack had always had more in common with Fox's mom. Neither could sit still for long, they both had a fiery, spontaneous spirit, and they shared a creative streak that Fox admired.

"Let's just say... Lynda's inspired me." Jack grabbed her arm, leading her from the aisle toward the front door. "Do you trust me?"

"Yeah, of course, but Jack—"

As they passed the aisles, Fox searched for Lynda, but she wasn't sure she'd noticed them in the first place. Even if she pointed her out to Jack, would they approach her? Would Lynda care to say hello and catch up? Maybe their time together hadn't meant much more to her than some extra spending money. Maybe she'd even found them annoying. The sensation of sadness filled her as she realized so many of the things she'd considered meaningful were often uncared for by others, like their childhood homes, or their families' traditions together ceasing over the recent years.

Fox noticed her own somber expression in her reflection off the glass door as she opened it. Jack grabbed her hand and pulled her out into the lot.

"Come on. We have to get you to work." Jack practically skipped to the truck. "The sooner you're at work, the sooner I can work on our costumes, and the sooner I can pick you up and we can celebrate this Halloween in *style*."

Jack started the engine, and they backed out of the parking lot while Fox dug through her bag. Not checking on her aunt's text in the store had been easy, but with a fifteen-minute drive to work, the suspense was killing her, and the not knowing was even worse. She had to check.

Fox gripped her cell phone tightly, staring at the screen as a lump formed in her throat. "Your mom texted me."

"What'd she say?" Jack asked, focusing more on checking out the town's pumpkins and ghost decorations hanging from the lamp posts out her window.

Fox read the texts aloud as they merged onto the main road in the direction of Haskin's on the outskirts of town.

Aunt Loralee: *Hey honey, I'm sorry for what I'm sure seems like short notice from me. The offer we got was cash, and it's all finalized, so we need to focus on finding you a new place. I've emailed you some listings of apartments in town. I know Jack would be more than happy to have you stay with her if those don't pan out right away.*

Aunt Loralee: *We're on a thirty-day close, and movers will be coming by next week to start packing. Jack hasn't texted me back yet, so when you're talking to her, could you let her know she has a week to get the rest of the things she wants before we put them in storage? Thanks for working with us, honey. Your uncle or I will be back on the 15th to figure out the rest. Moving is always stressful and we'll get through this together.*

"Wow." Jack slipped her aviator sunglasses on. "That's faster than I'd imagined."

Fox tossed her cell phone into her bag and took a deep breath. "I imagined it. It was so nice that they let me stay after I lost the modelling job, but between the rent I've been paying them and not finding anywhere else yet that would work around my current full-time hours, I haven't had enough time to save for the new place on my own. It's so expensive here—everywhere. How can single people afford it, never mind those with kids—"

"Hey, may I remind you that we finally have the chance to live our dream of having a place of our own, just you and me, together again, finally?"

"It's not that easy." Fox sighed, leaning back against the headrest, then tilting her face toward the window and away from Jack.

"How? Tell me what's so hard? I'll help you pack—I have to take my stuff anyway. We'll do the whole move together. You'll get a job, eventually—"

"I have a job *here*." Fox turned to her. "My doctor is here. My dentist is here. My father's grave is here. I love this town. We grew up here, Jack—"

"I know"—she raised her voice—"and I was fine leaving, exploring something new. It was easier then, but now *I* don't even have a home to come back to. I get it. It's like it's all slipping away."

Maybe she did understand.

"Exactly, but *you will* have a place to come back to. My new place. It won't be the same, but I'll rent somewhere in town, and you can come and stay with me, and we can still do everything we love, right here."

Jack sighed, using her knee to steer as she pulled her hair into a quick ponytail. "We could do that anyway. If you get your license, you can come back and visit every Sunday. It'll be a long drive, and I'll come too, whenever I can. You can still have your dentist here, but maybe you could switch doctors..."

"This is Ontario, Jack. I'll be on the waitlist forever!"

"Fox—"

Fox shook her head and leaned in toward the empty middle seat. "I have friends who still don't have doctors. Costa's mom only got hers because of her condition—and if she'd had a doctor before, maybe they'd have diagnosed her Parkinson's sooner—"

Jack threw her hands up before resting her head against her hand, cradled on the open-window ledge. "Then keep your doctor. Come back here and see her when you need to, like I do. I'll drive you."

She'd left Fox with no more excuses to make. Jack was right—they could make it work, but Fox didn't want to. She could admit that. She wanted to stay in the home she'd always known. What was so wrong about that?

Fox sighed. "I'm not like you. I can't just pick up and leave on a whim like everybody else in this family besides my dad. I want a homebase, Jack. I want stability, and I *could* make that anywhere, sure, but I *want* to stay here. Doesn't what I want matter to anyone?"

Her body trembled as she pulled her leg up to her chest. She turned to look out her window, letting the cool breeze whip her red hair across her face as a blur of trees passed before her eyes. She closed them and took a few deep breaths as the music got louder, because that's what Jack did when she wanted to tune everything out, even her own thoughts.

They remained quiet for the rest of the drive. As they pulled into the Haskin's lot, when she'd normally reach for her seatbelt buckle, an overwhelming feeling of dread kept Fox still. She didn't want to get out on that note. Ever since her dad's death, she'd promised herself to never leave anyone she loved when angry, because she never knew if she'd see them again and have the chance to make things right.

And there was something else—another anxious feeling swirling in her stomach as Jack parked in front of the doors.

Someone was out there with her last night, and she was pretty sure they hadn't been caught. She'd have heard. Someone would have told her. She didn't want to go to work. She didn't want to leave Jack.

"I don't—" Fox started.

"I've got things to pack." Jack kept her stare straight ahead at the windshield. "I've gotta go."

Fox grabbed her bag and hopped out of the truck. She'd barely closed the door when Jack turned the radio up, blaring Fox's dad's music to drown out anything she could have possibly said to make things right or to stop her from leaving. Fox stepped away from the truck, and Jack took off.

10

The field of tall grass across the road from Haskin's absorbed the golden glow of the early evening sun as it sank toward the horizon. The final scheduled recreational vehicle return of the day was due in five minutes. Costa rounded the counter to join Fox, and she turned her attention to the screen, waiting to see if the system would begin adding a late charge before the customer walked through the door. She kept three tabs open, each one an apartment from her aunt's list she was interested in seeing. All three were the cheapest available, and still too expensive for her to be considering.

Costa leaned back against the counter by her side, cracking open his orange can. "I don't know about tonight."

"The party?"

He nodded. "I already feel guilty about not being able to hand out candy with my mom tonight."

Three more minutes.

She turned away from the screen. "I get it. Listen, it's

almost eight. By the time you got home, I bet the porch light would be out, and she'd be watching TV."

"I just feel like I should be with her, but when I told her I was coming right home after my shift, she told me she'd be able to put herself to bed, and that I should take it easy tonight, go out, and live a little." He rubbed at the short, thick beard around his jawline and took a sip of his energy drink. "Which makes me feel even *more* guilty that she's so aware of the impact her disease has on my life instead of realizing I *want* to be home with her when I'm not working. I *want* to spend as much time as I can with her. She doesn't deserve this."

He stared out the big front window at the field across the street, his lips pursed, his hand clenched around the can.

"Hey. Neither do you." Fox turned her body to face him and sighed. "You do the best you can for her, and I think she might be sensing your burnout. You do a lot, Cos."

"I work two part-time jobs, and between that and dates with Kerry, I'm not there for my mom like I should be. But we have to eat. We have to pay rent. I—I've even considered breaking up with Kerry because I've started feeling guilty when I'm out with her. It's like, we'll be out having fun at mini-putt, or riding our bikes, or just down by the water, and then there's this guilt that comes up that I'm not there for my mom—and what happens if she's needing me, 'cause you know she won't call and interrupt me. She's stubborn. So, either I wish I was home with her or I wish that she felt better so she could be out like me, doing fun activities. Before I know it, the rest of the date night is ruined. I can't win, you know?" He cleared his throat and shook his head, downing more of his energy drink. As he swallowed, Fox waited to see if there was any more he wanted to share. "I didn't want this to turn into a pity party, okay? I just don't think I should go tonight."

Maybe that was part of his pattern with the women who came and went so quickly from his life. He felt too guilty to be spending time with any of them, but maybe, too lonely to stop dating.

"I'm not feeling so great about it, either..." She took two steps back and leaned against the wall. "Hey, if you ever need any help, you know I'm here, right? I'd really like to meet your mom. Maybe next week, I could bring some dinner over?"

"Yeah?" Costa's eyes lit up as he faced her.

"Yeah, and you could invite Kerry, too. Has she met your mom?"

He shook his head. "Not yet. I haven't introduced her to anyone since Katie, the girl I was with earlier this year. I just want to wait until I know for sure this time, if that makes sense?"

"Of course. You let me know how many I should make for, and if anyone has any allergies..." She trailed off with her words, cocking her head to the side as the front door opened and a man in a baseball hat walked in twirling his keychain in his hand. She turned back to Costa. "Hey, you should do whatever you feel is right tonight, but... we can talk more about it around close, okay?"

Costa nodded and turned around, facing the

customer as Fox grabbed the computer mouse. The late fee had been applied.

"Hey, happy Halloween!" Costa smiled, his bright, white teeth on display as he nodded to the customer.

Despite all his struggles, he'd always seemed to compartmentalize and put them to the side. She'd imagined the weight he'd been under, but he'd never vented to her like that before, and she was grateful he chose to confide in her. The smile he put on for the people around him hid the growing pain and guilt he'd been dealing with, and she hadn't realized the severity of the extent.

"Brought back three four-wheelers." The customer stopped at the counter.

"Okay." Fox looked from the late charge on the screen up at the customer. "In just a sec, I'll meet you around the back by the warehouse. We'll have you go ahead and park the vehicles in front of the double doors. I'll direct you where to go, you'll give me the keys, and then you'll come back inside. Costa will settle your bill with you."

"Sounds like a plan." The customer nodded, cracking a small smile. "Thanks."

She clicked the mouse on the late charge and deleted it, turning to Costa. "Back in a bit."

"I'll hold down the fort," he said, still smiling widely.

The customer walked down the middle aisle toward the front door as she exited behind the counter and turned left down the long hallway toward the back.

She stopped at the closed door to the manager's office and knocked. "Kennedy?"

"C'mon in!" Kennedy called.

Fox pushed the door open. Kennedy sat on her swivel

chair behind the desk and raised her head from the latest Kiersten Modglin thriller she'd been reading. "What's up, buttercup?"

The cat ears she'd chosen to wear for Halloween glimmered with sequins in the fluorescent light above. Several long streaks of black eyeliner extended from the cute pink circle on her nose to her round cheeks.

Fox couldn't help but smile at the effort Kennedy had made as she stepped into the office. "Last return of the day's here. Three ATVs. I'm going out back to direct him—"

"And I'll be there in a jiffy to load 'em back up." Kennedy rested her book in her lap. "Hey, listen, after what security told me about last night, I want garbage taken out in pairs from now on."

Fox nodded, relief blooming in her lungs as she stepped backward, grabbing the warehouse keychain that was kept hanging by the door. "Thank you. Will do."

"Ugh, I keep doing that!" Kennedy shook her head, staring at the pink makeup on her fingers after she must have wiped her nose. "You okay? I heard you thought you saw someone following you."

Fox leaned against the doorframe. "I thought there was... I was honestly dreading taking out the garbage, so I appreciate the new policy."

Kennedy nodded and raised her book again. "I've got security coming tonight *right* at close. No funny business on my watch."

Fox released a little laugh and pressed her clenched fist against the door frame. "Okay."

"Let me know when you two are finished, and we can

close up. Don't rush. I want to get to the end of this chapter. I have to know what happens next... and I have a theory..."

Fox grinned and nodded, turning left down the hallway toward the glowing red exit sign. Her breaths grew short as she neared the back door she'd pounded against the night before. She reached for the metal bar handle and sucked a deep breath in before pushing it open. She squinted into the last of the setting sun, just to the right of the warehouse. Engines grew louder to her right, and along the side road, three riders on three ATVs were followed into the lot by someone in a burgundy SUV. Fox stepped out and looked down for the heart-shaped stone to prop the door open. Another bigger rock sat beside the door, and she kicked it into place. She scanned the surrounding area for the heart-shaped stone, but as the customers approached, she jogged over to the spaces before the warehouse doors and began waving them over, pointing to each of the three spaces.

They took turns parking in the designated slots in front of her, revving their engines, no doubt enjoying the last of their rentals. They dismounted one by one, pulling their helmets off. The customer seemed to have brought his children. Two others, a man and woman about her age, waved a thank you to her before getting into the SUV with a woman behind the wheel—maybe their mom.

Fox's family had rented from Haskin's Great Outdoors Rentals for most of her life, her father having been an outdoor enthusiast. For a moment, she remembered joining her parents as they dropped off the canoes they'd rented, using the truck to haul them. That was before they'd decided to purchase two of their own. The end of a vacation or season was always bittersweet, but they'd created so many memories—camping, swimming, and canoeing together.

Her dad had taken her on countless camping trips in the summers in Ontario, Canada. They'd pitch a tent, and on the trips where it was just the cousins and her dad, she and Jack would wake in the early-morning hours, needing to relieve themselves. They got cold so easily as small children, always shivering as they stepped—their feet or shoes sliding—along the wet, dewy grass. They'd wander into the darkness of the brush with a flashlight and return to the tent, shaking, the chill of damp air seeping into their bones. Each time, her dad would tell them, it's always coldest before the dawn.

Later, Fox would hear others saying the phrase differently, replacing "coldest" with "darkest," but even when they did, she'd always think of her father as he tucked them back into their sleeping bags. He'd said the phrase, giving them hope as he reminded them that it wouldn't be long until the sun would warm everything it touched.

The family pulled back out onto the road in their SUV, rounding the building to the front lot again. Fox took a deep sigh as they disappeared.

Did they realize how lucky they were to be going on adventures as a family? Did they realize just how fleeting life was?

She turned to the warehouse and slipped the key into

one of the double doors, twisting it until it unlocked, and then the other.

Where is Kennedy? Probably lost in her book, as usual.

She grabbed the handle to the first door and walked it open most of the way before returning to the other to do the same. As she released the second handle, she heard a noise behind her and turned back toward the shop. The lot was empty, the back door still propped open by the rock. Another noise echoed from inside the warehouse, and she swivelled around as the singular side door to her right eased to a close.

She took a few steps back, scanning the side of the building as a deep-orange streak grew along the horizon in the trees behind the warehouse. No movement.

Did someone get inside? They'd have to have the key.

She walked toward the open warehouse doors, squinting into the darkness around the side door. With so many vehicles, small boats, racks of canoes, kayaks, and even some farming equipment, she wouldn't be able to see someone easily. Too many hiding spots.

She took one step into the warehouse, then another.

The long, fluorescent bulb in the back flicked on, followed by the middle, and then the first just above her as she turned to her immediate right.

A dark figure approached from the shadows. Fox stumbled back, her breath caught in her throat.

The fluorescent light reflected against Kennedy's cat-ear sequins as she emerged from behind the shadow of some boxes stacked by the side door.

Fox caught her breath. "You scared me!"

"Oh no." Kennedy laughed. "I'm so sorry."

"Where did you come from?" Fox handed her the keys. "Why did you go in the side door?"

She squinted behind her at the singular door.

"I went around front to say hi to Dottie. It was her family who returned these." She nodded behind Fox to the ATVs. "She's an old friend of mine. Anyways, speaking of the side door, last night when Luke called me, he asked if the side door to the warehouse was always kept locked. I told him it was, just like the sliding barn doors. I wasn't sure if somebody here was forgetting to lock it, so I wanted to check for myself."

"And was it?"

She nodded and held up her keychain in her other hand. "I had to use my key to get in."

Fox took a full breath and joined Kennedy as she walked to the first ATV. "So, why did Luke ask that?"

"He said he noticed a light left on in the warehouse on his second round of the property. I guessed either you, Scott, or Elisha forgot to turn it off after returning something. He found the side door unlocked. He said the light might have caught someone's attention, and if they came snooping around, it would have been an open invitation for someone to take what they wanted in here. Nothing was missing—I double-checked myself. Who was the last one in here last night?" She mounted the ATV.

Fox rested her hands on her hips. "I don't know..."

"Well, with the door unlocked, and a light left on, I have a feeling some people haven't been as diligent as they should be. We've gotta pay attention to the closing routines. I'm planning a team meeting to remind everyone." Kennedy started the ATV. "You both start closing duties, okay?"

She nodded, taking a step back as Kennedy drove the first ATV into the warehouse.

Fox slipped through the back door, leaving the rock in place behind her. She returned the keychain to the office and walked to the shopfront as Costa returned to the counter from stocking bucket hats on the wall.

"Saw you deleted that late charge." He grinned, taking a sip from his orange can. He swallowed and licked his lips. "How come?"

She hadn't made a conscious decision as to why she'd done it. It might have been because they were relatively new customers she hadn't seen before, and she wanted to make sure they had a good experience and returned. It might have been because he was only a few minutes late, and she didn't believe that warranted an extra charge. But it was probably because...

"Sometimes people just need a break, y'know?" She leaned against the end of the counter. "How are you doing? Do you want to continue that last conversation we had while we close up?"

Costa squeezed the can in his fist, crunching it as he shook his head. "I've just decided I'm going to go home and be with my mom."

He tossed the can into the recycling bin beneath the counter, and Fox gathered the garbage bag beside it.

"Wanna put the new bags on while I gather them up?" She nodded to the can. "Kennedy says we're to take the garbage out in pairs from now on."

They gathered the garbage from the front and the washroom.

Fox smiled at Kennedy with a bag in each fist as she passed her office. "Need yours emptied?"

Kennedy barely glanced up from her book. "No thanks, buttercup."

Fox lingered in the doorway, wondering how long the new garbage-pair mandate would last before she continued down the hallway. Costa waited at the back door.

"You okay?" Kennedy's voice echoed down the hallway.

"All good!" Fox called back as she reached the door.

"What's up? Why'd she ask that?" Costa pushed the door open, and they stepped out into the dim lot, the last of the colour fading from the sky into a deep, brilliant blue.

She realized he hadn't heard about the night before and filled him in as she placed the big rock between the door and the frame.

"Well, if Luke didn't find anything, there either wasn't anything to find, or they got out of here when they saw security. Doubt they'll risk coming back."

The person following her could have been in the warehouse, trying to steal something, and been startled when they'd heard noises from the dumpster bin. Maybe they'd even tried to leave and hadn't realized they'd been following her.

She pushed the dumpster lid open, and Costa swung his trash bag in easily. She did the same, and although the *bangs* and *clangs* felt tangible, abrasive, and jarring, causing her to clench her teeth throughout, no other noises came. No coughing or clearing of the throat. Fox took a deep breath and led them toward the back door.

"Oh, hold up, I've just gotta close this."

She turned as Costa jumped up and sent the dumpster lid slamming back down. "There's raccoons out here who'd love the chance at your leftover pizza crusts. I can't believe you don't eat them."

Fox grinned and shook her head. "Only if there's dip—"

A flash of white emerged from the dark shadows of the trees to the left of the warehouse. A figure in a mask. *The* mask?

Fox squinted and pointed at the figure, hissing, "Cos."

Costa jogged to join her side, looking in that direction. "What?"

Just as they'd emerged, they stepped back into the shadows of the trees, but she could still make out the white mask. Her lungs fluttered as she tried to breathe and goosebumps spread across her arms.

"Fox, what is it?"

"There! Don't you see the mask?" *The mask the killer wore*, but she couldn't say it. "The mask like Ryan wore."

Costa squinted toward the trees, and she turned to him, desperate for him to acknowledge and validate what she saw. When he looked back at her, confusion lingered in his gaze.

"Fox, I'm sorry." He turned back to the trees. "I don't..."

The figure in the mask darted to the side, toward the back of the warehouse.

"Come on," Costa shouted, grabbing her arm. He led her to the back door. "We're not staying out here. Crazies out here wearing that mask trying to scare people."

They reached the back door, and she slipped inside without looking back. Costa kicked the rock and closed the door behind him.

"That was freaky," he panted. "You saw *that* last night?"

She shook her head, passing him, walking down the hallway to the office. "They weren't wearing a mask last night. I would have seen that. You can't hide so easily in a white mask..."

The office sat empty, Kennedy's book closed on her swivel chair. Fox rushed toward the front of the shop.

"Hey, where—" Costa called, footsteps thudding down the hallway behind her.

"The front door!" she shouted.

11

The clacking from the keyboard alerted Fox to Kennedy's presence as she reached the shop front. Costa caught up as she slowed beside the counter, scanning the dark aisles.

"Everything okay?" Kennedy asked, turning back and forth to look at them.

"We saw someone out back wearing a mask," Fox said, confirming they were alone.

Costa stopped beside Kennedy as she reached the end of the counter. "It was that skull mask that guy wore. The guy who killed that girl in front of her dad."

"Piper?" Kennedy craned her neck back and turned to Fox as she kept her eyes on the front window. "Is that who you saw last night? Why didn't you mention the mask?"

No movement by the window. She had to lock the door.

"No, it was someone different, I think. No mask last

night." Fox took a deep breath and strode toward the middle aisle.

"Security should be here soon..." Kennedy called.

Fox paced down the middle aisle. Outside the window and just off the curb, a group of people waited, bathed in the red glow of the store sign—including the figure in the white mask.

Kennedy gasped, just behind Fox. "It's him!"

Fox jumped, glancing over her shoulder before looking back at the window at Jack.

"Jack?" Fox called through the glass as the group stood, staring at them.

"We've been waiting for you to close up," Scott called.

The man in the mask began to take it off. Ryan's messy brown hair caught her attention before he revealed his smug expression.

"You really shouldn't play pranks like that about something so horrific," Kennedy said as she passed Fox and opened the door for them. "Ryan Cherry, that mask was a *terrible idea. Just horrific.*"

"Why, thank you." Ryan laughed and sauntered into the store. "Nice cat ears. Elisha's meeting us there. Turns out, we get to meet her mystery man. Hey, you guys aren't in your costumes yet. I hope you brought them."

"I did, but man, I don't think I'm coming." Costa joined Ryan's side and shoved his shoulder. "You shouldn't be creeping around, scaring us like that!"

"What?" Ryan scoffed, craning his neck back as he held up the mask. "You loved it last night!"

"Yeah, well, tonight's different. You can't go around scaring Fox like that—not after what she saw last night."

"Bullshit," Ryan said, turning to Fox. "This is *exactly* the right night to go around scaring people."

"Watch your language while you're here, buttercup." Kennedy sighed, shaking her head as she walked toward the back counter.

Costa shook his head and pursed his lips, taking a few steps back away from Ryan. "Listen, I have to go home tonight. I'm not coming to the party."

Ryan stepped forward and wrapped his arm around Costa. "I bet you've got a sick costume, and you've been working so hard. I think you need to chill, have a drink, maybe smoke a little. Your mom'll be fine. You're always there for her, and you were just telling me she thinks you work too hard."

Costa sighed, running his hand through the pile of fluffy curls on his head.

Headlights shone through the glass, catching their attention. The white security car pulled into the lot.

"Perfect timing," Ryan shouted, turning his attention to Kennedy behind the counter. "Have I told you how cute your costume is? Hey, what do you say you let them go early tonight, Ken?"

"I'm not leaving Kennedy here alone," Fox said.

"I'm not alone. Luke's here," Kennedy called, her attention focused on the window, the screen glowing on her face in front of her. "You guys already took care of the tough stuff. I'm just going to count the cash. I'll be fine. You all go ahead and have a good time."

Fox turned to Jack, but she and Scott were whispering and giggling by the front door. Why hadn't Jack told Ryan not to try scaring her?

Fox walked back to the counter, lowering her voice. "Kennedy—"

"Listen, I don't need a babysitter. Security'll make sure I get out safe, and I mean, if you take Ryan with you, you're practically removing the headache for me." Kennedy winked at her with a small, genuine smile. "I'll be fine, buttercup."

She was right about Ryan. If he insisted on creeping around with that mask on, she wanted to be as far away from him as possible, too. Had he known what she'd seen out back the night prior? Probably, and he'd probably tried to scare her on purpose. Maybe Jack *had* tried to stop him. He never listened, anyway.

Fox glanced over her shoulder at him as he marvelled over his mask, and then caught Jack's eye. Jack who, despite the tension between them, was still waiting, wanting to spend what little time they had left together that weekend.

Fox tapped her palm against the counter. "Thanks, Kennedy. Will you text me when you're home safe?"

"If it makes you feel better, of course I will. I'll even let you clean the washroom next time you close."

"Perfect." Fox winced before laughing with her. "Don't forget to text!"

She returned to the group. "Alright, I'm ready." She turned to Costa. "Kennedy says it's fine to go. Are you going home or coming with us?"

Costa sighed and massaged his neck. "I'm going home."

"What?" Ryan scoffed, shaking his head.

"I *said,* I'm going home." Costa's authoritative tone was admirable. "And I'm putting my mom to bed, and then I'm putting on my costume, picking up Kerry, and meeting you guys there, alright?"

Ryan laughed, raising his hand and slapping it against Costa's back. "Nice. Sounds great. When you get there, you tell Goldie I took care of your drinks."

A mix of emotions ran through Fox as they walked outside. On one hand, she was pleased and relieved to hear Costa was coming, but on the other, she was frustrated at the satisfaction he'd just given Ryan after she thought he was standing by his own choices, unswayed by others' opinions.

Ryan unfolded his mask, ready to put it over his head as Luke approached from around the hood of his car.

Ryan opted to use one hand to shake Luke's. "Hey, buddy, I see you decided to work the shift instead of blowing it off on Smith and joining us."

Luke smiled confidently. "Some people have responsibilities and obligations they take seriously." His stare fell from Ryan's face to the mask in his hands. "Oh, come on. You got one of those?"

"Sure did." Ryan laughed and pulled it on.

"Seriously?" Luke squished his expression—half disgust, half disappointment. "Why am I surprised?"

"Because I keep things interesting. I'm not predictable like you." Ryan laughed from behind his mask.

Fox knew it wasn't all smiles under there. She saw it in his eyes from time to time and heard it behind the laugh he used to cover up his embarrassment, yet he kept making the same choices. And honestly, Luke was right—he hadn't grown as a person at all in the time Fox had known him, and nothing should surprise them anymore. Everyone kept giving him a pass, and Costa had just given him exactly what he wanted again.

"If predictable means keeping my commitments to my wife, saving for our future family, providing for them, and giving them a beautiful life... kinda like your dad does"—Luke's dry tone lowered to a more serious inflection—"then you're right. I'm predictable. Have fun at your party. You all be safe."

"Whatever." Ryan shrugged and walked past him.

As they dispersed to their vehicles, Fox hung back. "Hey, Luke, could you make sure Kennedy gets to her car safely tonight?"

He nodded with a slight frown. "I'm sorry I didn't find anyone last night. I guess Kennedy let you know about the unlocked side door to the warehouse? Besides the light that was left on, there was nothing suspicious. Nothing missing, either, I'm told. I'll make sure she's safe. Did something else happen?"

She sighed, shaking her head. "Just Ryan and that mask."

Luke leaned in closer. "Listen, he was one of my best friends, and he doesn't really mean any harm, but he also doesn't think things through either. I don't know if he's stunted emotionally, or if he's just lazy, but I look at him and I remember what we were like back in high school. He's still that guy, and..." His chest heaved as he lowered his voice. "I know you all hang out after work, and it's good to get along with your co-workers but... You *are* the company you keep, y'know?"

Fox nodded. She'd witnessed the slow fade of their friendship. Ryan spent more time with their group than he used to before, when he and Luke would hang out with other friends their own age. She'd never blamed the distance Luke was putting between them on him. It was Ryan's fault, yet she still couldn't help but feel for him when people attacked his character. There was more to him than his immature stunts and selfish attitude. Luke knew it, too, but he didn't have time to waste on Ryan if he wasn't going to change and do anything about it anymore. He'd said as much when he implied his wife, then girlfriend, suggested they spend less time together.

"You be safe." Luke passed her and opened the front door. "Hey there!"

"Hiya, buttercup," Kennedy called back as the door closed and he twisted the lock behind him, giving Fox one last nod.

Fox joined Jack by the front bumper of her dad's truck in the dark lot where she stood with Scott.

"You ready?" Jack asked, her tone light, but the heaviness behind her stoic expression stirred the anxiety in Fox's stomach.

Fox nodded and walked to her door.

"Oh, hey," Jack said, and Fox turned, realizing she was speaking to Scott who was following her. "Do you mind riding with Ryan? It's just I have our costumes in the middle there..."

Ryan walked to his car in the front lot, mask still on, pulling the hood of his black sweater up over the white plastic. Costa parted from his side and walked toward his own car. Scott's car was nowhere in sight, and she wondered if Jack had picked him up and driven him there.

"Oh, sure, no problem. I'll see you guys there," Scott said.

"Hey, wait, where's your costume?" Jack asked him.

He tugged at the collar of his green, plaid shirt and then at the sides of his red, corduroy coat. "You wouldn't recognize me without my axe. It's in your truck."

Axe? Was he Jack Torrance from *The Shining*?

"Heeere's Scotty!" he called, his voice echoing in the lot.

"Woooo!" Ryan turned back toward them in his creepy mask and howled into the night.

Jack smirked and shook her head, waving him off as she opened her door. Scott jogged to catch up with Ryan.

"See you there," Fox called to him, opening her door and hopping inside.

"Hey!" Ryan's muffled voice called before Fox had a chance to close her door. "Don't worry, Foxy, I'll protect you from the masked murderer!"

It was difficult to distinguish if he'd said "masked" or "axe."

Fox slammed the door shut, shaking her head. "He's always been such an asshole, but now this mask? Too far."

"Yeah, I know. I'm surprised you still put up with him." Jack pulled out of the parking spot, and Fox pushed the big garbage bag over a little so her work bag would fit on the seat. "I can't imagine what Piper's dad's thinking tonight... if he sees anybody wearing the mask."

Fox's stomach muscles clenched as she imagined the pain of having people in your own community wearing something the man who killed your daughter in front of you wore. Maybe Luke and Jack were right. Maybe it was time to leave Ryan to his own devices and stop seeing him outside of work.

"Does he get this is real life?" Fox sighed. "Or does he think it's all just some joke, as long as it doesn't directly affect him?"

Although the question was rhetorical, Jack shook her head, driving past the guys who'd seemed to wait until they got out safely first—no doubt at Scott's insistence. They took a left turn at the exit instead of the right they would take to get home.

"You know where you're going?" Fox asked.

Jack nodded and turned the radio up a bit. They rolled their windows down, inviting the smoky, autumn scent into the truck, driving along the winding back roads of Auburn Hills. It was one of the first times in their adult lives that they'd shared an awkward silence. Also, one of the first times Fox had held fast to her own decision instead of caving and catering to Jack's.

Fox grabbed her red apple from her bag and checked her phone before slipping it back in and sliding it onto the floor between her feet to give the garbage bag the room it seemed to demand. She crunched into the apple and sweet juice sprayed the corners of her lips. She licked them and chewed, eyeing the garbage bag.

"So..." Fox grabbed the opening of the bag and swallowed. "Thanks for making our costumes. What did you decide on?"

A little smile graced Jack's lips, but she didn't look over at her. "Remember that movie we used to watch with Lynda about that girl and her sister? She becomes a werewolf, and her sister has to save her, but—"

"*Ginger Snaps*," Fox exclaimed, turning to her. "We haven't watched that in ages!"

"I know! I got white hair chalk for whichever one of us wants to be Ginger, so we can get our front pieces. I made a bit of fake blood for around her mouth, too." She reached her hand into the garbage bag and fished out two white charms, dangling from the necklace twine in her grasp.

"You made the matching necklaces?" Fox grabbed them, admiring the detail Jack had put into the white, oval clay charms, remembering more of the movie.

"Mhmm. Not the exact same as theirs, but I worked with what I had. And listen, I know Brigitte's costume isn't as unique, but I figured whichever one of us was her could wear my camera I got for school around their neck with a thick turtleneck sweater I grabbed from my mom's closet."

Jack would be Ginger—it was obvious she wanted to be. It was the more unique, revealing costume. After Jack went to the effort of putting together something she knew would be so meaningful, Fox was happy to let her have it.

"This is awesome," Fox said with laughter and glee, pulling the dark green turtleneck from the garbage bag.

"And whoever goes as Brigitte gets to stay warm. You wanna be Ginger?"

Jack smiled. "Sure."

Fox leaned back against her seat. "I never meant to get snippy with you. I haven't told you how grateful I am for your offer to stay with you—"

Jack's big, warm brown eyes met Fox's. "Not *stay* with me. Live together. Rent a place that's both of ours—mine and yours. Maybe it'll just be while I'm in school. Maybe it won't even last that long. I just wanted to take the opportunity to be close to you again, like we were before I left."

"Hey, I want that, too." Fox pushed the turtleneck back in the bag. "It's just hard because I can't imagine leaving everything behind here."

Jack played with her grip on the steering wheel, fixing her hands at ten and two, and then midnight. "Do you... do you feel like everyone's leaving you behind?"

Fox shook her head. "No. Well, kinda, but it doesn't bother me. I think I'm more upset that our family doesn't find as much meaning as I do in our traditions and the places we've created a life—and they literally created lives in. It's just not so easy for me to let go of that, and really, why should I? It all means something to me. You all mean everything to me."

Jack turned to her, giving her a look of empathy, her features softening before she turned back to the road ahead. "You're everything to me, too. To our family. No matter where everyone is, it doesn't mean we love each other any less."

Fox twisted her apple around, inspecting it for punctures and bruises. "I don't expect people to stick around for me—I really don't. You're all doing what makes you happy. Auburn Hills just happens to make me happy."

"That sounds terrible, Fox." The rasp in Jack's voice was always accentuated when she was stressed. "I don't want you to feel like no one's choosing you or prioritizing you—"

"And you shouldn't. No one should. We all have goals to achieve and lives to live, and I feel like I'm finally being pushed to start my own and..." She turned to Jack, bracing herself for a hurt expression. "I want to stay here."

Silence grew between them as a haunting, Halloween-themed song played. Fox took another bite of her apple.

"Is that your final answer?" Jack asked, her stoic expression remaining as she shook her head. "You won't come with me?"

Fox swallowed her mouthful and released a deep breath. *I don't want to hurt her.* She inhaled, filling her lungs with smoky, autumn air. "Can we just have tonight? Just one night where I don't have to think about what I'm losing and what you're trying to gain, and we just realize we have each other?"

Jack nodded, her stoic expression melting away. "We can definitely do that. We can have tonight."

12

Staring out the window as they drove past the oldest neighbourhood in town, Fox couldn't spot a single child as wind whipped through the trees, stripping them of their remaining colours. Her dad's radio station played haunting Halloween songs from various popular movie soundtracks, with a few rock classic covers sprinkled in. She and Jack sang along as they turned the next corner onto Old Watermill Road.

The truck's headlight beams became searchlights on the old country road, illuminating a group of college-aged people. One wore a werewolf mask, a woman wielded a chainsaw, and a man had on a black cape, blowing majestically behind him. As they drove past, he pushed his fingers into his mouth, adjusting his fangs. Vampire.

"I guess they're going to the party." Jack squinted as she looked down the car-lined street for the house. "I guess they all are."

"I think that chainsaw's from *Evil Dead*." Fox turned

over her shoulder, focusing on the woman who held it. "Unless she has a mask, and then, it'd be from *Texas Chainsaw Massacre*. I don't see a mask..."

"Maybe it's not from a movie." Jack glanced over her shoulder, then turned to Fox with a sly grin. "Since when does a woman need an excuse to wield a chainsaw, anyway?"

Fox released a light huff of laughter, nodded, and continued watching as the group crossed a large lawn toward the old, two-storey home with a sad-looking pumpkin beside the door. Whoever put it out hadn't taken the time or care to make it a jack-o'-lantern.

"Hey, when was the last time we carved—" Fox started.

Someone in a skull mask walked in front of their truck on the road ahead, then stopped in the middle, staring at them. Chills crept up Fox's back, tingling her enough to make her shake them off as she realized the skull was missing the bottom row of teeth.

"Is that Ryan?" Jack asked.

This one wore a black hoodie like Ryan, but it was darker than his—Ryan's was slightly faded in comparison. The figure simply stood, staring at them.

"Why's he just standing there?" Fox whispered.

Jack honked her horn, but the figure didn't jump. Their shoulders seemed to rise slightly and fall, but Fox couldn't tell for sure. The dark figure nodded to them before walking across the road, in no hurry to get out of their path.

Jack pressed her foot on the gas pedal. "That was weird."

"If that was Ryan, he's taking this creepy act too far..." Fox said, but she didn't believe her own words.

It wasn't Ryan. Somewhere deep inside, she knew it, and just then, she wondered if the figure in the mask at Haskin's might not have been Ryan either.

Her cold hands turned clammy as she wrung them. "Hey, when you got to the shop, was Ryan already waiting at the front, or...?"

Jack slowed down as she approached an empty spot adjacent to the house. Another couple approached, walking past them hand in hand as a zombie bride and groom.

"No, I got there first with Scott." Jack took a wide turn, backing into the spot with ease. "He texted, asking if I could pick him up because he wasn't finished with his car yet. Ryan showed up after."

Jack shifted into drive and twisted the wheel before inching forward, positioning herself directly between the cars. She reached for the keys in the ignition.

"When you say 'showed up,' did you see where he came from?"

Jack hesitated with her hand on the keys. "What?"

Simultaneously, the song on the radio ended, and as Fox opened her mouth to explain, a special news bulletin notification sound caught her attention.

"Tonight, while our breaking story is unrelated to the terrors of Halloween, it's directly connected to the horrors facing Auburn Hills since this September when forty-one-year-old Slate Cornell and twenty-year-old Piper Cornell were taken hostage, abducted from their home, and brought to the dark, desolate corner of

Palmerston Park where Piper was murdered in front of her father—"

"I can turn it off," Jack said.

Fox shook her head.

"... witnessed by Auburn Hills resident, Samuel Merrick, who as of today has been reported missing by his long-time partner, Candice Thorpe. She's accepted our invitation to come on and send a message to Samuel, or whomever he may be with, in an effort to ensure his safe return. As our listeners may remember, Merrick was walking his dog along the path of the park that night when he spotted the scene and alerted authorities—a heroic effort the local police believe may have saved Mr. Cornell's life. We've got a picture of this man posted on our website, and we'll have more information after our interview, so please reach out or alert the Auburn Hills police of his location if you see him."

"You okay?" Jack asked.

A song began to play, slow and haunting.

Fox bit her lip and turned to Jack. Her wide eyes stared at Fox, filled with concern. She twisted the volume dial slightly to the left, leaving them with echoes of laughter and a faint throbbing of bass coming from the party house.

"I just keep thinking..." Fox took a deep breath. "There's something about that mask. I wore one—not that one of course, but I know what it does for you. It protects you, provides anonymity, but it also adds an element of mystery and intrigue—enough to make people fascinated with recreating and even wearing it, and in this case... Jack, if that witness hadn't seen the mask... we might not have even known anything about the killer, never mind had a sketch of it. I heard Slate Cornell didn't cooperate with the police in terms of details. They said he was too traumatized, so it was *that* witness who provided the information on how to find the killer. And now, Ryan and these people are wearing it—"

"So, wait. Was Slate Cornell withholding information that could help them catch his daughter's killer?"

Fox shook her head. "We don't know everything. I'm sure the police have kept some details private, but the word is, he wasn't very cooperative with them. Apparently, at first, they thought he was having some sort of mental breakdown, but then the psychiatrist cleared him, so..."

Jack shook her head. "Look, I can't imagine going through what he did, but you'd think he'd want to do everything in his power to catch the killer..."

"He was traumatized—"

A knock at Jack's window made them jump. Scott laughed, stepping back to allow Jack room to get out.

"Let's just go and try to have some fun, okay?" Jack grabbed the keys and bag.

Fox slipped her cell phone into her pocket and hopped out, rounding the truck to meet them. Scott jumped onto the side, reached into the bed of the truck, and produced his axe from it.

"There's so many people here," Scott said, holding up his axe and pretending to chop something with it. "You guys need a minute?"

Jack held up the bag. "We just have to put these on,

and we'll be ready."

Scott glanced over his shoulder. "Ryan's waiting for us at the door."

Ryan stood beside the sad pumpkin—maskless—talking to a guy in the open doorway.

"At the door? What? Is there a guest list?" Jack scoffed, pulling her jacket off, revealing a tight, cut-off shirt.

Scott laughed, looking away in a possible attempt to give them some privacy. "Apparently, he's had neighbours call the cops on him before."

Fox frowned as they looked around at the empty field across from the houses and squinted down the road to barely see the neighbours' bungalow in the distance. "He said his neighbours have got it out for him, and when the police came, they said he was violating some sort of fire code? I don't know. Ryan just said the guy's keeping it to people he knows this year."

Jack pulled the turtleneck from the bag and handed it to Fox. Fox pulled the sweater over her head, the soft fabric adding extra warmth, immediately calming and protecting her against the wind. Jack handed her the camera, and she pulled it over her head, taking the matching necklace next and pulling it over Jack's head. She did the same for Fox, grinning.

"You need any help?" Scott turned back to them. "Can I carry anything? Need me to bring your drinks in?"

Jack dug through the bag. "Oh, I brought a four-pack of Fox's favourite cider, but I'm not drinking tonight. Gotta drive."

Scott nodded, his smile fading. "Oh, gotcha. Yeah,

I'm not drinking, either. Hey, how about *I* drive you guys home?"

"Oh, no, don't worry about it." Jack pulled the white hair chalk from the bag and handed it to Fox. "I love alcohol, but sometimes it does *not* love me. It's not a big deal."

"Thanks, though, Scott." Fox nodded to him before running the chalk through the front pieces of Jack's hair. "Oh yeah. This works. This is going to look amazing!"

"Well, really, it's not a big deal." Scott shifted his weight from one foot to the other, swinging the axe from side to side. "I didn't drive here, and Ryan can get a ride home with Costa and Kerry. One of them will be sober, I'm sure."

"You're very sweet." Jack smiled as she tapped some of her homemade fake blood against her lips. Fox pressed the tip of her finger into the blood and traced a line from the corner of Jack's lips, just past her beauty mark, toward her chin. "Really? You sure, Scott?"

Scott nodded with a grin. "It's your cousin's Halloween celebration weekend together. Of course I'm sure."

Fox finished up with the blood, nodding with approval. Jack stepped toward Scott.

"Thanks." Jack hugged him. "You're the best. Okay, ready! I should have brought some beer."

"Oh, I'm sure they'll have lots." Scott beamed, starting across the street. "It *is* a kegger after all."

Fox nodded with a laugh, and they followed.

"Fox, is that you?" A deep, familiar voice called to her from the bottom of the driveway.

13

A man with long, wavy brown hair to his chin and brilliant hazel eyes stopped a few feet ahead, staring at her. His arm was wrapped across the shoulders of a girl about her age, dressed like Tinker Bell.

"Dylan," Fox said.

Jack swivelled her head to look at her cousin, but Fox didn't take her eyes off of Dylan. The way he stood with the girl beside him, so protective in his stature, evoked a surprising amount of jealousy.

While she'd worked for Crescent Moon Studios, he'd been their primary photographer. He had an amazing talent for capturing the right mood for the client, and a way of making the models feel comfortable in his presence. They'd started flirting last September while on set for single shoots, and that had led to some time spent together outside of work after Jack had left for college. She'd been surprised the first time he'd asked for her real name after one of their shoots, having only ever referred to her by a number in the past. He'd known he was breaking the rules when he contacted her personally, asking to go see a movie at the local drive-in. Although flattered, she turned him down politely three weeks in a row before finally giving in to the temptation. Exchanging personal information with anyone at work was forbidden in her contract, but she'd wrongly assumed Dylan was a worthy exception.

Despite his determination to see her, and his efforts to get to know her, Fox had often wondered if the chemistry she'd felt had been one-sided. He'd never made a move on her, and he'd always treated her like a friend. During their brief time together, he shared some photos with her for side projects he had, asking for her favourites to put a portfolio together. After he'd expressed an interest in nature photography, they'd rented a canoe together and she guided him on his first trip down a local river.

By that winter, they'd gotten so close she decided to tell him how she felt. She wanted to explore their connection. If he only thought of her as a friend, at least she'd know, instead of fantasizing about something more. Before she could, Dylan quit his job at the studio, stopped answering her calls, and left her on "read" after his final text.

Eight months since she'd seen him—or maybe it was closer to nine. It had taken months before she'd stopped wondering about him, at Jack's insistence. After the spring, when the company closed down, she never expected to hear from him again.

As he stood before her, his arm wrapped around someone new, she wished he'd walked right past without acknowledging her like she'd have done to him.

"It's been a while. How've you been?" Dylan asked, stopping in front of them.

Tinker Bell shyly glanced at them before looking down at the pavement, swaying a little. Jack wrapped her arm around Fox, pushing her toward the lawn and front door.

"Great," Fox quipped, and muttered under her breath, "couldn't be better."

"You *look* great." Tinker Bell swayed in Dylan's arms as they moved to cross the road, stumbling as he caught her. Fox walked forward, Jack guiding her toward the door with a hand on her back, and stared down at her huge turtleneck. No makeup, hair a mess from the wind whipping through it on the way—Tinker Bell must have been sarcastic. From behind her, the young girl's voice came again. "What? Uh oh. Am I in trouble?"

Fox turned to look over her shoulder, but Jack pulled her close and forced her forward onto the grassy lawn. Music blared from the front door, still not loud enough for the neighbour to hear, but she wasn't sure how Ryan and the guy in the trench coat with a hook for a hand at the door could hear each other.

"Hey, perfect." Ryan waved them over. "Goldie, these are my friends from work."

Goldie nodded at them as a loud crash came from inside.

"Goldie's gonna kill you," someone called, followed by laughter.

Goldie rolled his eyes, pulled a joint from his

pocket, and waved his hook-hand, welcoming them inside. He closed the door behind them, twisting the lock.

"You okay?" Jack whispered. "That was wild. You haven't seen Dylan since—you know..." Jack raised her brow.

Fox shook her head no, licking her lips and turning toward the locked door. Why had Dylan even stopped to talk to her if he was on a date with someone else after ghosting her completely? He could have just kept walking, and she'd never have noticed him.

"That girl he was with... What was she, a fairy?" Jack pursed her lips, deep in thought. "She looked drunk—"

"Hey!" A guy hopped off the couch in the front living room in a full red jumpsuit costume, bumping into them as he passed to give Ryan a quick handshake before bounding down the front hallway. Maybe he was dressed as the Tethered from *Us*.

Fox and Jack followed Ryan in the same direction, past a few party-goers into the large, farmhouse-style kitchen. A ping-pong table sat where a kitchen table might have been, with red Solo cups arranged in position for a game of beer pong.

"Kegs are there." Goldie pointed to the counter by the sink with his hook-hand as more rumblings came from the basement. He turned to Ryan. "Snacks over there. Don't touch anything that looks expensive, okay? I gotta go see who broke my shit, man."

Ryan nodded to him as he left, opening a door just off the kitchen in the hallway that led to a descending staircase. Their host disappeared into the darkness. "I told you, you better not be getting into my parents' wine! You asshat!"

Ryan filled four red Solo cups on the counter from the keg.

"Oh, hey, I'm not drinking tonight." Scott held up his axe in protest.

"I'll take his." Jack wiggled her brows at Scott and laughed. Ryan handed her two beers. "I bet I can drink one faster than you, party boy."

Ryan laughed. "No way. Let's go."

Before Fox could advise against it, they both chugged their beers in the middle of the kitchen. Amber streams ran down their chins, and pink bubbles of beer mixed with fake blood dripped onto Jack's chest. They finished at relatively the same time, pointing at each other and laughing.

"Oh-kay..." Fox slid a can of cider from the box and turned to Scott. "I'm sticking to these tonight."

He smiled and nodded, turning his attention back to Jack, as usual.

Ryan wiped his chin with the sleeve of his faded black hoodie and rounded Fox to the ping-pong table. "Who's up for a game? We can do teams!"

"Hello!" Elisha's voice called from down the hallway.

In an effort to get away from Ryan, Fox eagerly accepted the distraction and slid past the party-goers in the hallway again. She made it to Elisha and hardly recognized her. Wearing all black, her orange face stood out in contrast—her mouth, nose, and eyes painted black like the carvings of a jack-o'-lantern. A tall man, also in black with similar face paint stood beside her, his arm around her waist. Fox recognized his crew cut, now slicked back away from his orange face, and his once scruffy jawline appeared smooth.

"This is Fox, oh, and that's Jack!" Elisha called past her. Jack joined her side. "Jack, meet *jake*-o'-lantern!" Elisha laughed and shook her head. "Guys, this is my date, Jacob."

Jacob nodded and smiled politely, but he didn't laugh at Elisha's play on words. Instead, he pulled her closer. Fox and Jack both said "hello".

"Happy Halloween," Jacob said, his voice was rougher than she'd imagined.

Fox could just make out the corners of his real, upturned lips. *Were you the one following me at Haskin's?*

"Happy Halloween," Jack echoed.

"Hey, I'm not sure if Elisha mentioned it to you," Fox said, leaning in to be heard over the music. "Last night, there was someone out back at Haskin's after we closed. Was that you?"

He nodded. "Yeah, I parked around the side. Elisha didn't tell me where to park, so when she didn't come out, I drove around to the front lot."

Elisha looked up at him. "She saw someone following her outside, around the building."

So, she hadn't asked him about it, and she still wasn't.

"Following her?" Jacob craned his neck back and shook his head with a chuckle. "You don't think it was me, do you?"

"Of course it wasn't." Elisha beamed, wrapping her arm around his waist.

Maybe not, but he hadn't specifically denied it.

"Nice face paint!" Jack shouted over the music and turned to Elisha. "Did you do it?"

"Thanks." Elisha nodded, her eyes wide, seeming to marvel at the jagged lines that comprised Jacob's chilling smile.

"She did great. Where are the drinks?" Jacob asked. "I'll get us some."

"Thanks, babe." Elisha squeezed his arm.

Jack pointed over her shoulder to the kitchen, and he passed them.

"I didn't even know you had a boyfriend," Jack whispered, pulling Elisha into the living room and out of the high-traffic area—and the earshot of their other friends.

Fox followed.

Elisha turned to Fox. "I usually tell you everything, and I know you tell each other everything, but I've had to keep this hush-hush."

"What?" Jack asked, exchanging an equally confused and intrigued expression with Fox. "Why?"

Elisha looked around them, then over her shoulder, and whispered, "Can you both keep a secret?"

She hiccupped, and they all laughed, with Fox and Jack nodding yes.

Elisha leaned in closer. "He works at the college. He's a professor there."

"What?" Jack's eyes opened as wide as her smile. "Your college? That's *scandalous*."

They all laughed. The white of Elisha's teeth shone in high contrast to the black lips surrounding them as she smiled, tucking the front pieces of her short bob behind her ear.

Elisha took Fox's hand, leaning in closer as she whispered, "It *is*... because... he's married."

Fox frowned, letting go of Elisha's hand. "*What?*"

Elisha glanced over her shoulder again, squinting through the dark living room to the bright hallway with the zombie bride and groom making out by the front door. "It's not official yet because he promised once I graduate, he'll leave her and we can finally be together."

"Finally?" Fox balked. "How long has this been going on?"

No wonder he hadn't seemed thrilled to be introduced to her friends. She was surprised he'd agreed to come out with her at all, but the face paint made more sense. Still, if any of his students were here, there had to be a chance they'd recognize him. They were taking a risk. Maybe it was exciting for them. At that thought, Fox took a step back.

"Like I told you, just a few months. I met him over the summer. I didn't even know he was a professor. I swear. It wasn't even serious, but then once we discovered our close proximity, it became this... *temptation*."

"Sounds hot... minus the wife." Jack turned to Fox, eager to see if she'd be able to hide her disdain for the situation. She turned back to Elisha quickly. "Let me ask you this. When he tells you he'll leave his wife, do you actually believe this jerk, or do you realize he'll be hiding you away like the dirty little secret you are to him for as long as he can?"

Maybe it was the fact she'd practically shouted it to

be heard over the music, or maybe it was the alcohol that made her words come off so harshly. Jack wouldn't normally have been so brash.

Fox wanted to tell Elisha she'd broken the rules herself, violating the terms of her contract to see Dylan outside of work. She wanted to warn her that while it felt exciting in the moment, it wouldn't be worth it, especially in her case.

The smile disappeared from Elisha's face for the first time since she'd arrived. "He's a really good guy, honestly. Jacob's trying to do the right thing—"

Fox shot Jack a look that said "stop" and took Elisha's hand again. "Elisha, we just want the best for you. I know it feels exciting right now, but a guy who's going to lie to his wife until it's more convenient for him... You can do better. You *should* do better."

Elisha's eyes opened wide as she raised her brow. She swallowed hard before lifting her chin and taking a step back. "Yeah, I didn't think you'd understand. I should have kept it to myself. I should go find him."

"Elisha," Fox said, but Elisha had already reached the hallway, and even if she heard her, she continued on. "Ugh, well this is great."

Jack took the white, matching charm of Fox's necklace in her hand. "It's a mistake. She'll learn."

"She's going to get hurt."

"I know." Jack sighed and took a swig from the liquid remaining in her cup. She wiped her lips with her hand afterward and left pink remnants on the back of it. Fox wiped at Jack's mouth, tidying the mess of fake blood. "Listen, that's not our problem right now. Our problem is, we aren't having fun yet, and I know how to solve it!"

Jack nodded toward the kitchen, and Fox followed. As they reached the kitchen, Jack led her around a corner into a dark room with strobe lights and dancing party-goers in a myriad of costumes. Fox held Jack's hand, and they danced together, jumping around the room and laughing as they bumped into others—or were bumped into.

"This," Jack shouted in her ear, "is what I needed. I miss this."

"Me too!" Fox shouted.

Jack finished the rest of her beer and swallowed, licking her lips. "I miss *you*! That laugh!"

As the song changed, and they danced to an old favourite from their high school days, Fox downed the last of her first cider. The stress of the day melted away, and as she lived in the moment, she never wanted it to end.

"Let's get another drink!" Fox shouted.

Jack grabbed her free hand and swung it around in the air. "I wanna keep dancing!"

"Come with me," Fox shouted. "It'll just be a sec."

Jack released her hand and handed her a Solo cup.

"Okay! I'll be right back!" Fox took it and rounded the corner, stopping at the line for the keg. The host in the trench coat turned to her. "Just one, please."

He nodded and stepped aside as she filled it up and grabbed another can of cider from the box on the counter where Scott had left it, returning to the dance room as quickly as she could without spilling. As she walked through the dancing groups, a witch bumped into her. She lost her grip and spilled some of the beer on her outfit.

"Sorry!" Fox shouted.

The witch waved her off with a smile and kept dancing. Seconds of searching for Jack through the crowd of dancers turned into what felt like a minute. She pushed past the group they'd seen at the beginning and came face to face with someone wearing the skull mask again —this time, all bottom teeth accounted for. This person hadn't made it look like the specific one used by the town killer, but the way they stared at her made her flee into the hallway. She looked back and forth, with no Ginger in sight. She crossed past the front door and into the living room, where they'd been before with Elisha.

Elisha stood with Jacob, talking to a couple dressed as Batman and Catwoman. As Fox walked past, Elisha made eye contact and looked away quickly, back to Jacob.

She wondered if Elisha had actually seen her and was purposely avoiding her—and if she'd continue to while at work. Panic rose inside her chest as she approached the kitchen, finishing a full lap of the main floor without any sight of Jack. Someone in a skull mask stood in the doorway, blocking her from entering —no bottom teeth. Their dark, black sweater had the hood up. She felt them staring down at her from behind the material before the eye sockets, although she couldn't see their eyes to confirm it. It felt like the one who stood in the middle of the road when they'd arrived.

"Ryan?" The words came out in a meek, breathy question.

A question she already knew the answer to... and the chills across her flesh told her to run.

She turned around, pushing through the dark, crowded living room, desperate to put distance between them. As she spotted Elisha and Jacob, the sharp, crisp, upturned smile on their jack-o'-lantern faces turned menacing. A vibration at her side stopped her. Her cell phone. She swivelled around, squinting through the darkness, unable to see the skull mask.

"Jack?" she called out.

A cough came from behind her, and she jumped. The werewolf tapped Fox's shoulder and leaned in closer with his furry face and fangs. She stumbled back, away from him, and laughter from a group behind her blended together with the music. It was all muddled. The panic became trapped in her chest as she spun around in circles, looking for anyone they knew, surrounded only by the faces of monsters and strangers.

14

He peered through the crack of the door in the wine cellar, into the dark room made even darker behind the sheer, black material of the eye sockets on his mask. It would have been completely black if it weren't for the white glow of the TV, lighting up the faces of the couple on the couch across from it. He wrapped his arm around her, all cuddled up as *they* watched the screen, and he watched *them*.

If they thought they were clever, tricking everyone by stealing away for some time alone, they were wrong. Anyone could find them; all it took was a little time and attention.

Maybe they *wanted* to get caught. He didn't think so, but then, he was sure they were used to getting away with what they wanted. People thought they could just get away with their misdeeds, and dirty secrets, and their crimes. Most of the time, the man on the couch could. Most of the time, there was no one around to stop him from taking what he wanted and leaving the rest behind, never to be a consideration for him again after the brutal fallout left catastrophic consequences for others.

He'd make him remember.

And then, he'd make him pay the toll twice.

The woman giggled, pressing her hand against the man's chest.

He stepped back, away from the crack in the door, pulling the rope from the front pocket of his hoodie. It was almost time, and he didn't have long—not nearly long enough to teach them the worst lesson he'd ever learned.

No matter how tightly you hold on, you lose the ones you love.

Sometimes, they slip away peacefully, while others are ripped away with such cruelty that the loss, and the anger, and the pain are too much to bear.

They'll take a life without a second thought, but they won't take accountability for it.

He pulled the rope tight, clenching each end in his fists before curving it and shoving it back in his hoodie. He reached behind him, to his back pocket, his fingers pressed against the hard handle sticking out of it. It was something he'd used before and relied upon. Something that would put the pain back where it belonged.

It was almost time.

15

Bass vibrated through Fox as she stumbled down the hallway toward the kitchen. She pressed her phone to one ear and her finger to the other to drown out the music and the beer pong players hollering up ahead. *Pick up, Jack.* The call went to her voicemail, like Jack's had to her moments ago. She stopped at the counter, leaning against it for stability as anxiety threatened to burst from her chest.

"Hey, Foxy, whatcha doing?" Ryan stepped beside her and grabbed a Solo cup, pressing the lever on the keg.

She jumped, clutching her cell phone. As frustrating as his familiar face was most of the time, it was a welcome sight in the sea of strangers. She licked her lips and ran her fingers through her hair, taking a deep breath as she focused on his unfaltering smile.

"No... better question." He shuffled to the right, away from her, and tried the lever of the next keg as he raised his voice. "Why don't you have a drink in your hand?"

Where had her drinks gone? Had she set them down

in the dining room when that man in the skull mask blocked her way to the kitchen?

"I can't find Jack," she shouted, grabbing his shoulder to pull herself closer to his ear as she picked up on the scent of mint and citrus. "I need help."

He seemed to study her, pursing his lips as he frowned. Releasing the lever, he held out the Solo cup, offering it to her as if it was the help she'd asked for. How drunk was he?

She leaned in closer, taking another deep breath of mint and citrus from his hair. "Just help me find her, okay? We lost each other. She tried to call me, but I missed it. I can't reach her."

"Yeah, yeah." He waved her off and took a gulp of the beer. "Listen, if I help you find Jack, will you be my wing woman?"

She raised her brow. "Since when did you start admitting that *Ryan Cherry* needs a wing woman?"

He rolled his eyes and took another sip, then he shrugged as he gulped. "I'm not gonna help you find her for nothing. If I do it, I want you to help me with this one girl. She's not really responding to my charms. Shocking, I know."

She took a step closer, her eyes at his chin, staring up at him. "You help me find Jack in less than five minutes, and I'll do what I can for you with this girl. Deal?"

She extended her hand, and he smiled, shaking hers with a hot palm and tight grip before releasing it quickly. He took a long chug of beer. His smile reached his eyes as he peered down at her from behind the cup, then led the way past the beer pong table toward the back door. He walked with his shoulders back, his head high, easily forging the path through the beer pong players.

"What are you and Jack supposed to be, anyway?" he shouted over his shoulder.

"Ginger and Brigitte from *Ginger Snaps*. It's a horror movie we watched when we were younger." She stopped herself from explaining further, wondering if he was even listening to something that wasn't about him. She picked up the pace, elongating her stride to keep up with him past the back door. He was too eager, too focused. "Either you're desperate for my help with this girl," she called, "or you already know—"

They stopped by the large window beside the back door. Fox spotted Jack immediately, sitting at the patio table on the large, wooden deck, adjacent to the man with the werewolf mask up on his head. It was as if the music faded in the background, and Fox could hear her own thoughts again. He extended his arm, a joint pinched between his fingers. Jack laughed, shaking her head no.

Fox shoved Ryan's arm, keeping her eyes on Jack. "You knew! You jerk!"

Ryan took a drink, seemingly staring out the window at Jack, but Fox caught him looking at her reflection from his, smirking.

"There she is, safe and sound." He wasn't speaking as loudly; maybe the volume *had* decreased.

"You cheated." Fox turned to him, a small smirk on her lips.

What else could I expect? Wait, why isn't he wearing the

skull mask for the party? Did I see two other people with similar masks, or has it all been Ryan?

"Whether I knew or not is irrelevant. Wasn't part of the deal." He held his hand up, gently tipping his drink toward Fox, feigning innocence. "We had a bet, and we shook on it."

"You made a bet with the devil?" Scott laughed behind them, rounding the beer pong table with a soda can in one hand and his axe in the other. "What'd he win?"

Fox took one last glance at the man in the backyard with his hand on Jack's leg and spun around, planting herself in Scott's line of vision.

"Hey, umm, Ryan, you tell him"—she grabbed Scott's arm and circled him, switching places so Scott's back was to the window—"while Scott helps me fix the back of my costume."

"Oh, yeah, no problem." Scott rested his axe on the floor against the wall and handed Ryan his can. "What's the issue?"

Fox turned around and lifted her hair, pointing to her neck. "Do you see that clasp on the band of the camera? I think it's caught in my hair."

"Foxy here's going to help me land the girl of my dreams tonight, aren't ya?" He made a clicking sound with his mouth and chuckled gleefully.

"It's just the clasp, I think," Fox repeated, glancing over her shoulder as Scott pulled more of her hair to the side, giving the clasp his full attention.

"I *think* you're all good," Scott said, hesitating.

If he turns back around, he'll see Jack flirting with someone else. His night would be ruined.

"Scott—" she started, turning to face him.

"Hey, help me get some more drinks." Ryan wrapped his arm over Scott's shoulder. "Kegs are almost dry, and there's some secret backup cases of beer in the garage fridge."

As Ryan led him away, he didn't look back. Had he realized he was part of the distraction, or was it just a happy coincidence? She walked past the beer pong players to the back door. She had to get Jack and bring her back in.

A man in a clown mask and blue jumpsuit stepped in front of her, his back to the door, blocking her path.

"Happy Halloween," he said from behind it. "Can I get you a drink?"

"No, thanks. I was just going outside."

She reached for the doorknob, and the man took a step to the left, covering it with his back. "Need some company out there?"

She needed him to get out of her way. Fox glanced over her shoulder, but Ryan and Scott had already disappeared down the hallway.

She rested her hands on her hips, trying to take up more space. "Could you move, please?"

He stood still and pulled his mask off, revealing the sweaty face of a stranger smiling down at her.

She walked around him to the side, reaching for the doorknob. She'd get out there, even if she had to use the front door and take the long way. He stepped aside. He must have gotten the message.

A warm hand wrapped around her forearm, sliding down to her wrist, and she turned as the man pulled her toward him.

"Hey!" she yelled, twisting her wrist and snapping it away from him in one swift motion.

The man opened his mouth to say something to her.

"You got a problem, buddy?" Costa shouted from across the table, but it wasn't long before he was by her side. All the beer pong players stopped and stared. Costa turned his glare from the man he'd placed his body in front of back to Fox, who was rubbing her wrist with her other hand. "Oh, you've got a problem now."

"Not even worth it." The man chuckled, pulling his clown mask back on.

She grabbed Costa's arm and pulled him toward the door, twisting the knob. "Thank you."

They stepped out into the fresh, autumn air, tiny stars scattered across the sky above and beyond the fields behind the property. She walked across the deck and around a group who were smoking cigarettes.

"Glad I made it when I did." Costa followed her. "Where's everyone else? You okay?"

The patio table was empty, save for a beer can, a red Solo cup, and the charm from Jack's matching necklace resting on the deck beside the chair she'd sat on.

Fox bent down, grabbing the white, clay medallion. "Jack was just out here."

Costa walked to the wooden railing of the deck, scanning the yard and turning back to Fox. "Maybe she went back inside. She's probably trying to find you. Let's go in and see if we can find her."

She didn't want to go back in—and she didn't want to stay—but she took a deep breath and nodded as they walked to the door, side by side.

"All I wanted was to spend Halloween with her, have some fun, but now this… this isn't it." Fox stopped as Costa opened the door for her. "Thank you, and thank you for what you did there."

"Don't mention it." He nodded as she passed. "I was going to say I should have stayed home, but now I'm glad I came. What a slimeball. Literal *clown*. This is *not* my kind of party."

"Same," she muttered, although she'd never been one for any kind of big party, it felt good to share the sentiment of a level-headed friend.

The only one she'd been to since high school was in Jack's residence on campus during her first year of college, and she'd spent most of the time playing drinking games with Jack or in the bathroom, helping the other girls who'd gotten sick. She told Jack she was done with those types of parties. Jack understood, promising never to invite her to another one—a promise she'd kept.

Costa followed her through the kitchen, stopping before the basement door where they met Ryan and Scott coming back down the front hallway with a case of beer in Scott's hands.

"Hey, man." Costa nodded to Ryan and then Scott.

"You made it!" Ryan shouted. "Hey, where's Kerry?"

"She's catching up with a friend she saw out front." Costa peered around them, toward the front door. "She said she'd come find me, but after what happened with Fox... Just wait here a sec."

Costa put his hand on Scott's shoulder as he passed them, shuffling toward the front door.

"We're trying to find Jack," Fox shouted over the music.

"Again?" The music's volume couldn't hide the exasperation in Ryan's tone.

"What'd Costa mean?" Scott asked, readjusting the case in his grip. "What happened?"

"This guy in a clown mask grabbed me." She turned and looked over her shoulder as she muttered, "Creep."

Costa passed them again, rejoining Fox's side. "She's still out there. I told her I'd come back in a few. I don't really want to leave you alone in here."

"I'm going to check downstairs." Fox nodded to the open doorway. "If you guys find Jack, could you tell her I'm looking for her and to meet me out front?"

"Yeah, of course. I'll look, too." The strain on Scott's face grew. "I just have to put these in the kitchen."

"Come on, man," Ryan said, waving his hands. "Hey, clear the way! More beer! Make some room!"

Fox inched toward the basement door, and Costa followed. "I'm coming with."

"Hey"—Ryan's voice reached them as Fox and Costa descended the stairs—"remember, you owe me, Foxy!"

It echoed in the basement, where Fox heard two other voices before they rounded the corner to face the entertainment unit and the zombie bride and groom watching the big, bright screen. They squinted over at Fox and Costa. The groom gave them a look like they were intruding, with his arm around the bride before returning their attention to the screen.

To her right, a door was open just a crack, revealing a floor-to-ceiling rack filled with wine bottles.

"Jack?" Fox called toward the wine cellar.

"... never came home last night." The female voice came from the speakers of the sound system. And on the TV screen, a blonde woman with wavy hair and a green, plaid shirt stood in front of a house surrounded by trees, a microphone in front of her chin held by an out-of-frame interviewer.

Fox turned back to the cellar door. No answer. No other noises except from the TV. Fox looked at Costa, and he pressed his lips together in an apologetic smile, heading back for the stairs. Fox hesitated, watching the screen.

"And then this morning, I realized Pally—that's our dog—he hadn't been fed. Sam'd never forget to feed Pally. I had a gut feeling last night something wasn't right, but when he wouldn't answer calls or texts—and the neighbour hadn't seen him—I realized his dog bowl was empty, and that's when I called the police."

"Excuse me." Fox stepped beside the TV screen. The couple barely glanced at her. "Have either of you seen a girl with brown hair with white streaks down the front and some fake blood on her mouth down here?"

"Nope," the groom said without turning his focus from the TV.

"Hey, did you see that guy upstairs with a mask just like that one?" The bride nodded to the screen where they all focused their attention.

The B-roll clip of the woman in front of the house with her dog had cut away back to the station, where a journalist sat behind a desk and the sketch of the skull mask was imposed on the top-right corner of the screen.

"That was a clip from our interview with Candice Thorpe, the partner of Samuel Merrick who's been reported missing since late last night or early this morning. Merrick was the witness to the brutal murder of Piper Cornell, and he's been hailed as a hero who saved the life of her father, Slate Cornell. He was last seen by his partner on the morning of October 30th at their residence in Auburn Hills. We'll bring you the latest update on the victim of The Skull Masked Murderer, but first, a word from my co-host about the hotline to send in any tips you may have on Merrick's whereabouts..."

"Sorry." Fox raised her voice as Costa joined her side by the screen. "Neither of you saw the girl with the white—"

Costa leaned in. "These two wouldn't have seen that clown come in if he'd stood right in front of them. If she was down here, they can't help us."

She nodded and followed him back to the stairs, turning to the dark crack in the door and hesitating.

What if Jack is in there? What if she went in there to make out with someone, or she's passed out and can't hear me calling?

Fox took a step toward it, reaching out for the knob.

16

"Slate Cornell checked himself out of the Auburn Hills Centre for Mental Health Sciences earlier yesterday morning," The news reporter droned on as Fox reached for the door. "As more details about the victims are discovered, we bring you to the outskirts of Auburn Hills along a concession road leading to the city of Sterling Heights, where our reporter, Nim Lee, is on location."

"Jack?" Fox called, pressing her fingers against the door.

"A building where we learned the deceased, Piper Cornell, victim of The Skull Masked Murderer was employed. A company called Crescent Moon Studios, owned by the Kinmonts, two brothers..."

Fox froze and turned back, looking over Costa's shoulder at the screen. The reporter stood with a microphone in front of the abandoned studio. Fox could barely process her words. She never heard another soul besides

Dylan or Jack ever utter the name of the studio, and it felt *wrong* in the pit of her stomach on its own, never mind alongside Piper Cornell's. They knew about the studio— everyone would know. Piper worked there. She *knew* her? How was any of it possible?

"What if it was her dad?" the bride asked.

"You think the dad killed her?" The groom craned his neck so he could face her. "No way, the witness saw a man in a mask."

"Then maybe Slate Cornell went crazy. Maybe he went after the witness because he saw too much? Maybe he was in on it and hired..."

Fox did her best to tune out the couple as the journalist spoke, desperate for clarity. "As we continue to dive further into the case in hopes of aiding the local police department in the hunt for a masked killer this Halloween, I stand before the former Crescent Moon Studios, where I've just learned that Piper Cornell was employed until her recent murder—"

The studio had closed in the spring. Whatever facts the news station thought they'd had, they were wrong about that. Piper couldn't have been working there when she was murdered in September.

"So, do they think it was someone from her work?" the bride asked.

"Maybe." The groom looked over at Costa. "Maybe someone had a vendetta against her, and they went to kill her, but her dad was there..."

"This old, abandoned building seems like an unlikely place for a modelling studio, but could it be a front for another business, something more sinister?

Something that led to the demise of twenty-year-old Piper Cornell?"

How did they learn about the studio? Did I ever meet Piper? She needed to tell Jack what was happening—they needed to talk it through.

Fox turned around and shoved the cellar door open, revealing a dark room of walls lined with wine bottles. She stepped onto the damp, concrete floor. An open case of wine sat on top of the wine barrel in the middle of the room. Jack wasn't there. She wasn't there, and she needed her.

"Let's go," Fox ordered, her heart beating in her ears as tears pooled in her eyes.

The news station dug into Piper's history, and if they'd gotten as far as the studio, it wouldn't be long before they uncovered more about their modelling business. And when they did, would they find out who else worked for them? It was all supposed to be anonymous. *Did Piper tell someone about the company before she was murdered? How could they have figured all that out?*

She took the stairs in twos, Costa's heavy footsteps following her. Her stomach clenched at the feeling of being chased.

The news station didn't have all their facts straight. Maybe that meant she'd still have time before anyone found out about her pictures. Her legs shook and her stomach churned as she reached the hallway. What would happen if her secret was revealed, the pictures became public, and everyone knew what she'd done?

Emerging from the basement, Costa squeezed past her. "Hey, let's check the front."

She nodded, swallowing back tears. He started down the hallway, but for a moment, the world slowed down before her. She grasped at the neck of her sweater, tugging at it as she struggled for each breath. She had to get ahead of it all somehow. She needed Jack.

17

Fox raced down the hallway, bumping into someone in black. They turned, revealing their orange face with jagged, black paint lines—Jacob, Elisha's boyfriend. "Sorry."

"Sorry man," Costa called over his shoulder as he opened the front door, leading the way.

She stepped outside, the cold hitting her face as she hurried down the driveway, pulling her cell phone out of her jeans pocket to call Jack. As she slowed down, she spotted her brown hair with the white streaks. Jack stood by the truck with Scott, her arms folded over her chest, smiling as she spoke to him.

Fox stopped, remaining still in a moment of calm, quickly torn away by the distance between them. Dread filled her again; the tide rolled back in, leaving her drowning with the information she had.

"There she is." Costa tapped Fox's arm and nodded to the road. "And there's Kerry."

He pointed across the lawn, and they parted ways wordlessly.

As Fox rushed down the driveway to the road, Scott reached out to touch Jack's arm as Jack noticed her.

"Hey," Jack called to her, stepping forward out of Scott's reach as Fox jogged across the street. "What happened? Where'd you go?"

"Where did *I* go?" Fox grabbed Jack's arm and pulled her toward the bed of the truck and away from Scott before letting go. "The girl who was murdered? Piper Cornell. She worked at Crescent Moon Studios, too."

"She what?" Jack frowned. Her confused expression faded as she shook her head, as if to shake away the effects of the alcohol she'd consumed. "Why didn't you tell me—"

"I *just* saw it on TV. I don't think anyone knew until now." Except the Kinmont brothers, and maybe Dylan. "I've had this bad feeling ever since last night, with that guy following me at work, and now that I know she worked at Crescent Moon, too... I feel like there's this connection."

"You're empathic, Fox." Jack tilted her head to the side and rested her hand on Fox's arm. "You always have been, and I know you've been feeling for her. I don't think *anyone* feels safe with a killer still out here in Auburn Hills, and the skull masks aren't helping—"

"I want to leave." Fox caught her breath and dug into her pocket, handing Jack her clay charm she'd found on the deck. Jack frowned at it before her eyes opened wide. She grasped at her necklace where her charm would have been. "This was supposed to be a night for us to have fun, but you've been gone on your own, and then I saw the building on the news, and I don't know what's happening or why. I want us to go home—"

"There you are," Ryan panted, jogging across the street with Costa and Kerry following. At first, she hadn't realized Costa was wearing a costume, but in his black collared shirt and pants, and with Kerry's cami, jean jacket, her natural curls replaced with straightened hair, plus a stake in her hand, together they must have been Buffy and Angel. "What are you all doing out here?"

"We're leaving," Fox called to him, then turned to Jack. "We're going home."

"Hey, sorry the party's a little lame." Ryan stopped, resting his hands on his hips. "We ran out of beer too fast. We can get someone to go get some more for us. I'm talkin' the good stuff."

As Fox took a deep breath preparing to argue, Scott joined her side.

"Sorry. Your friend with the hook was cool," he said to Ryan. "But, yeah, I'm not letting anybody else touch them in unwanted ways. That's bullshit, man. I'm taking them home."

Ryan closed his mouth and pressed his lips together as he scanned their faces, speechless for the first time.

"I forgot my axe in there." Scott sidestepped and walked backward across the road. "Anyone remember where I put it?"

"You rested it on the wall by the back window when you were helping me. Remember?" Fox shouted to him, anxiously wringing her hands in front of her. "And could you hurry?"

Scott nodded and jogged back toward the house.

Jack rested her hands on Fox's shoulders and pulled her to the side, around to the tailgate. She turned her so they were face to face. The blood on her mouth and chin had mostly faded, leaving a pink stain on her lips. Her eyes searched Fox's as if she were trying to find a way to get through to her.

"I get how you're feeling, and I want to leave, too. You have every right to be upset. I'm sorry I wasn't spending time with you." Jack released her arms and lowered her voice. "Cooper's been trying to call me, so I came out front and told him to stop. Then, I tried to call you, but you didn't pick up. I was just telling Scott, I think the breakup's been getting to me. I saw someone in there that reminded me of Cooper, and... I just need to shut off my phone and be in the moment with you. Can we go back home, just our group, and enjoy the rest of Halloween?"

"Jack," Fox whispered. "That's all I wanted, but now..."

She sighed, remembering the news reporter outside the old studio. With a connection to the murder victim, and her reputation threatened, she just wanted to curl up in bed with Jack while she promised her everything would be okay.

Fox cleared her throat and turned to the group. "We're gonna head home."

"Y'know, you're onto something, Foxy." Ryan ran his fingers through his hair, pushing it away from his face as his eyes met hers. "We should definitely do the after-party at your place."

"We still have an hour left until midnight. An hour left to run amok." Jack grinned and grabbed her hand. "And the other stuff? We'll figure that out together. You *know* we will. I promise it's going to be okay."

Fox took a deep breath and squeezed Jack's hand.

"What's up, guys?" Elisha asked, tucking her hair behind her ear as she stopped between Costa and Ryan.

"Elisha!" Kerry shouted, pushing past Costa to give her a hug. "Love the face paint! Wow!"

"Hi, um, who are you?" Elisha asked, keeping her arms at her sides.

Kerry squeezed her and stepped back. "Oh, sorry. We met once before at the bar last month. Winburn. I'm Kerry, Costa's girlfriend."

"Oh, right, sorry. I've had a few drinks." Elisha shook her head with a smile and glanced over her shoulder. Jacob stopped on the front lawn across the street, staring at them. Scott darted past him, axe in hand, and crossed the street. Elisha cleared her throat, her gaze flicking to Fox and then Ryan. "Jake's just kinda done with this party."

"Us, too. We're going to their place, and you're driving." Ryan handed Kerry his keys before turning to Scott. "We can stop by my place and grab some booze if you guys want to grab some snacks on the way. Candy's probably super discounted right now—"

"I think Jacob and I are just going to go home." Elisha fished her keys out of her pocket, casting a glance at Fox. She pressed her lips together in a tight smile and shrugged. Was that supposed to be a polite apology? Fox couldn't take the tension between them—not with everything else she was dealing with. "See you guys at work."

Fox rounded the group and pulled Elisha aside. "Listen, I'm not trying to judge you. Trust me, there's too much of that in this world, and I'm not trying to join the critics. I just don't want you to get hurt."

"And I appreciate that." Elisha nodded. "I forget that not everybody will understand our connection. What we have is... I've never felt anything like it. I don't want to look back and have regrets. If this is a mistake, I've gotta learn it for myself. But you're a good friend, Fox."

Beyond the face paint, Fox recognized Elisha's confident expression. They were equally stubborn, and there was nothing more she could say.

"What do you say?" Jack called to Fox. The group formed a circle, letting Fox and Elisha in. "We go home, just our friends, have some good drinks, snacks, and maybe a little hot tub time? We'll take our minds off of everything and just have fun." Jack stepped into the middle of the circle toward her. "Give me one more chance to make this Halloween one to remember?"

She couldn't control whether her identity would be released—or her pictures. It killed her to even consider it, but just like Elisha, there was nothing more to be done. If she let this moment slip by, and pushed away her friends in favour of worrying, she'd regret it.

Jack leaned in and whispered. "Be my Lucy again?"

Fox cracked a smile and nodded.

"Yes," Costa shouted into the night. "Let's get outta here."

Kerry took his hand. "Yeah, those skull masks are

really creeping me out."

Elisha crossed the road, joining Jacob's side. Fox thought she heard him utter, "Let's go back to your place."

"Hey," Ryan called across the road. "You're not coming?"

Elisha's stare landed on Fox, her eyes slightly squinting as if she was trying to decide what to do. Fox crossed her arms, awkwardly hugging herself in the cold, giving Elisha a hopeful smile. Would she come with them, or take a risk on learning the hard way with her date?

"I think we'll skip it," Elisha called, resting her hand on Jacob's chest. "We're going back to my place to go watch something scary, right, babe?"

Jacob nodded and called, "Have a good night."

Costa waved to them. "Drive safe. Nice to meet you, man!"

Jacob waved back, and they walked to the brown car parked further down the street, closer to the neighbour's house.

"What did you think of him?" Ryan asked in a muted tone as Elisha and Jacob walked further down the dark road.

"Oh, I didn't get a chance to talk to him. I was just being polite." Costa shrugged, turning back to the group. "Did Elisha seem kinda off to you guys?"

Jack and Fox exchanged a quick, pained look of understanding.

"I didn't get a chance to talk to her," Ryan said, "but the guy wasn't drinking. I offered him a beer, so I guess she'll get home safe at least? Let's not waste any more time."

"You're all going together in Ryan's van?" Scott asked, stepping between Jack and Fox.

Costa kissed Kerry's cheek and pulled his keys from his pocket. "I'll take my car."

"Meet you guys back at the house," Ryan said, nodding. He clapped his hand against Costa's back before wrapping his arm over Kerry's shoulders. "Last to arrive has to streak through the backyard!"

Kerry laughed, and Costa punched his arm as they walked away. Scott took a step forward and turned to Fox and Jack.

"I promise, this night is going to get so much better," Jack slurred her words, pulling her keys from her pocket with her cell phone and handing them to Scott. "Take it all. I'm going to stay present with my Lucy. You really *were* my Brigitte tonight. I'm sorry."

Fox mouthed, *I know.*

"Oh, sure, okay..." Scott tucked her phone in his pocket before dropping his axe into the bed of the truck and fidgeting with the keys. "Hey, Fox, you sure this is okay? Me driving the truck? Us going back to yours?"

She didn't want to be around a bunch of people, but with four of her closest friends and her best friend spending the night, she felt a bit safer.

Fox gave him a quick nod and rounded the truck to the passenger's side. He didn't deserve to have her take out her frustration on him, and she'd ripped Jack away from him moments before, so she added, "It's just been a weird night."

"But it's about to be a great one because we're getting slushies on the way to use as mixers!" Jack opened the driver's side and hopped in, sliding into the middle seat. She shared a smile with Fox. Slushies were one of their favourite treats they'd walk to the corner store for most Friday nights in their teens. "And we'll light those big pillar candles my mom was saving for a special occasion, run the hot tub, and stargaze with some excellent drinks and some excellent people. Excellent, excellent."

Scott hopped in the driver's side.

"Could you stop at the gas station on the way?" Jack smiled at him. "You know the one that has slushies, right? It's the only other one in Auburn Hills with all the good flavours. Thanks so much for doing this."

"Of course." Scott pushed the key in the ignition, and as he turned it, she recognized a familiar song playing softly through the speakers.

Just hearing the music from her dad's favourite station began to soothe Fox. She rolled her window down and linked arms with Jack. Scott pulled out of the spot and drove past some party-goers on the street before making a three-point turn. Fox leaned her head back and put her arm out the window, slicing through the breeze created as he picked up speed. In the rearview mirror, someone in a skull mask stepped onto the road and stopped in the middle, seeming to watch them leave. She watched them until Scott made a left turn and they disappeared from the mirror as they merged onto the dark road ahead.

18

As they drove down the back roads, Fox and Jack sang along to the songs they knew. After some prodding from Jack's finger into Scott's side, he even joined them on one. Fox was pleasantly surprised to discover Scott's deep, warm inflection sounded even better when he sang. They parked beside the gas station and hopped out of the truck as Ryan's van sped down the road toward them, Kerry laughing away in the driver's seat. As they passed, Ryan turned in the passenger's seat and pulled his pants down, mooning them. Costa's car followed closely behind, giving them a few short honks of his horn.

Scott laughed, shaking his head as they walked toward the gas station door and he pulled it open, holding it for them. They entered the station with warm fluorescent light casting deep shadows from all the racks. Fox squinted, letting her eyes adjust to the yellow tint. They nodded to the attendant. He nodded back before turning his attention to the small-screen TV behind the counter across from him, the remote clutched in his hand.

Jack and Fox rushed to the back of the store and stopped at the ice machine, examining the slushie flavour options.

"Wanna mix our favourites?" Jack asked. "And then make them guess the flavour combos?"

Fox nodded with excitement as Scott grabbed a few bags of chips from the middle aisle, shaking his head at them with a grin.

"Happy Halloween, folks!" the attendant called to them. "Going to a party?"

"Leaving one." Scott stepped out of the aisle to address him properly as they grabbed cups and started filling them with their favourite flavours: grape for Fox and orange soda for Jack. "Busy tonight?"

"Surprisingly quiet," the attendant said as they stuck their first drinks in a tray of four and began filling two more with different concoctions. "People haven't been in much since the kids finished shellin' out."

Scott nodded, holding up the chips. "Can I leave these on the counter?"

"No prob." The attendant nodded and turned back to the TV as Scott rested them on the counter.

Jack tried to lift the tray full of drinks, but it wobbled, almost tipping over. Fox grabbed it, tipping it the opposite way until they rested it back on the machine safely. Both of them erupted in a fit of giggles. Fox pushed her to the side and lifted the tray, carrying it to the front counter and resting it beside the chip bags.

"Cool costumes," the attendant said.

Fox smiled politely, although there wasn't much left of their costumes, especially with Scott's axe back in the truck. She questioned his comment silently to herself as a shot of the reporter from earlier on the TV panned to a large house behind her. It wasn't the same house as the missing witness, Samuel Merrick. This one was huge, sectioned off from the neighbour's well-manicured lawns with police tape.

"Almost ready." Jack nodded to the attendant and turned to Fox. "What else? Why don't we each get our favourite ice cream and some root beer, and we can make floats?"

Fox nodded absentmindedly, watching the screen. "Sure. Go for it."

"Scott, you like floats?" Jack called to him at the back, and took a few steps down the aisle toward him.

He chuckled. "I don't mess around like that with my ice cream. Hey, let me help you out, there."

"Could you turn that up?" Fox stepped up and leaned against the counter, nodding to the TV.

"Oh yeah, sure. Brutal. Just absolutely brutal. " The attendant grabbed the remote, and as the volume rose, the acid gurgling in her stomach bit at her throat.

"... two currently unidentified victims were found here, early this evening, when a call was made to the police by someone known to one of the victims of this tragedy unfolding before us on Halloween night."

B-roll close-up shots of police tape transitioned to a wide shot of the pristine yard. A white, plastic voter support sign stuck out against the short, bright-green:

Re-Elect William Bonetti for Mayor of Auburn Hills. The shot switched to a stretcher with a body bag, panning to a wide shot of paramedics and police officers hoisting it into an ambulance without flashing lights.

Scott and Jack flanked Fox at the counter, their hands full of treats.

"Police found two people stabbed to death in the basement of a house over on Roberts." The attendant nodded to the screen, his eyes fixed on it. "They just did an interview with one of the neighbours. Apparently, a woman who owns a clothing store downtown lives there on her own, but the neighbour said she saw a black sedan come and go sometimes, and it's parked out front there. Could be the victim. Could be the perpetrator."

Three murders in less than two months, and one missing man involved. Fox's legs wobbled beneath her as she used the countertop for support. She shared a connection with Piper. Could it just be a coincidence? It didn't feel like it.

"That's terrible," Jack whispered. "When did it happen?"

"Today," Fox muttered. "Earlier tonight. Did they say anything about a man in a mask?"

The attendant pursed his lips and shook his head. "Not that I could tell. Like that skull mask on TV? You think it's connected to that girl who was murdered? Damn... Coulda been. Didn't even think about it..."

An officer walked down the driveway and ducked under the police tape, shielding his eyes from the flash of cameras.

Scott set his items on the counter and watched the

screen. "I know that street. There's Richie Row. Some of the wealthiest in Auburn Hills live there."

"That's right." The attendant began scanning and bagging their items. "All those folks have money on Roberts, and you'd think they'd have security systems..."

Fox tried to tune out the attendant and focus on the reporter.

"We're waiting on an official statement from the police," the journalist said, before she threw it back to the anchor at the station.

Fox's breathing grew short as she waited for more news about Crescent Moon Studios. She clenched her jaw and fists, preparing to hear her own name or see her own pictures on the screen.

"Thank you, Nim. We've just learned that in a recent development, Slate Cornell, victim of The Skull Masked Murderer, is wanted by the police for questioning regarding the disappearance of witness Samuel Merrick."

Her dad? But why?

"Hey." Jack nudged her, tilting her head toward the door where Scott waited with three bags and their tray of drinks in his hands.

"Let's go," Fox muttered.

They met Scott at the door. He pushed it open for them with his back against it. Jack went first and Fox turned over her shoulder for one last look at the screen.

The sketch of the skull mask filled it. There was something they couldn't quite capture with it—the eyes. In the sketch, they were drawn as dark shadows shaded in because the only witness saw it from a distance.

In person, the sensation of their eyes staring at her

from beyond the two black shadows disturbed her to her core.

19

Wind whipped through Fox's red hair as she lost herself in thought, staring out at the blur of trees. The dark, winding back roads, lit only by the moon, fostered a nervous tension growing inside of her. If they could just reach home, she'd have the security it always brought her.

"Hey," Jack whispered, leaning close to Fox's ear. "Whatever's happening, whatever loose connections you're making, don't overthink it, okay?"

Fox nodded, only because she couldn't rationally explain why she felt so close to danger. The link between working with one of the killer's victims made the threat of her identity being revealed seem more manageable in comparison. Jack swayed the other way, leaning closer to Scott. He smiled down at her as she tugged at the collar of his plaid shirt and laughed.

As they passed a farm, a dark gray cloud rolled over the waning moon above.

"Isn't that beautiful?" Jack asked, leaning over Fox for a better look out her window.

"Haunting," Fox muttered.

Jack grabbed one of the cups from the tray between Fox's feet and took a sip, offering one to Scott. "See if you can guess the flavours."

Scott sucked on the straw and nodded with a wide-eyed pout, leaning his left arm out the window to rest on the edge. "Tastes like a cold headache."

Jack giggled and elbowed Fox gently. "No one's going to guess."

Fox raised her brows and tried to force a smile as they passed the field of corn, disappearing between the tree-lined road toward the middle of town.

Fox's phone vibrated in her pocket, and she slid it out.

Jerk Alert: *Just leaving my place now. Bringing the good stuff. Prep yourselves to give us a show!*

Fox sighed. "They're leaving Ryan's now."

"I think we'll get there just before them," Scott said, as the song on the radio changed. "Not that I'm streaking either way."

The familiar melancholy melody caught her attention—one of her dad's favourites that she hadn't heard in years. She exchanged a knowing grin with Jack. Jack leaned forward and twisted the dial, blaring the rock song. She put her slushie back in the tray, and Jack sang along to every word. For a little while, Fox lost herself in the memories of driving with her parents in the truck on the way to camping trips, and with Jack when she'd first gotten her driver's license, and just her dad when she was younger, going on an adventure. Always on an adventure. Others called them errands or tasks but her dad had the knack of making whatever had to be done that day a little more special.

The truck bobbed up and down with a jerk, and they stopped singing, veering to the left. Fox grabbed the door handle, and Jack linked her arm with Fox's. Headlights from a car shone around the corner in the left lane.

"That was some pothole." Scott gripped the wheel with both hands, turning to straighten them out. "I can't..."

The approaching car continued to speed their way.

"Scott!" Jack shrieked.

As the car passed on the left in the opposite direction, it swerved slightly to get around them. A long, blaring horn sounded as they drove away. Fox inhaled a shaky breath, turning in their direction, wide-eyed.

"We have to get over. I lost control—" Scott started, but they bobbed again.

They slowed down, but the jumping and jerking continued. Fox couldn't let go of the handle to steady herself. Scott twisted the wheel, steering them toward the tree-lined shoulder of the road, onto the gravel. A scraping sound of metal accompanied them until Scott stopped.

"Was that a tire?" Jack asked, her voice clear of the slippery texture of alcohol for the first time since they'd left the party. "Did one of the tires just pop?"

"I don't know." Scott shifted into park and took a deep breath, releasing the wheel before turning to them. "I think that would have been more of a shock. We might have driven over a nail, or some glass, or it might not be the tire. I'll go look, okay? You guys stay here."

Jack nodded, turning the volume down as he opened his door.

The spare tire her dad had always kept would get them out of a jam if that's all it was. Fox could change it herself. But what if it was something worse? What if a whole part had fallen off?

Fox pulled her arm loose from around Jack's as Scott closed his door behind him. Fox opened her door and hopped down onto the gravel on the side of the road. If something was wrong with her dad's truck, anything more than just a tire, she needed to know. She needed to fix it. They had to.

"Hey." Jack slid into the passenger's seat. "Wait for me."

Fox stopped between the trees a few feet away from the edge of the gravel road, their peppery, minty scent hitting her as she checked out the tires on her side of the truck. Both seemed full, normal. She rounded the hood to Scott's side, where the back tire seemed lower than the front, yet still round.

"Think something punctured it?" Fox asked, joining his side. "Did we drive over something?"

"It's not the tire." Scott bent down beside it. "I'm pretty sure it's the axel."

"What happened to the axel?" Jack asked, joining Fox's side. "Is that bad?"

It sounded bad—expensive.

Scott sighed. "I thought I told you to stay in the truck."

Fox bent at her waist, peering into the dark wheel well. "What's wrong with the axel?"

He looked up at her and then back in the wheel well. "I'd have to take a better look to be sure, but when it breaks, you can't steer properly anymore."

He pointed past the tire, and Fox crouched, leaning against his arm as she squinted into the darkness. "I don't know what it should look like."

Her dad had taught her a bit about his truck, but she wasn't even in high school yet when he passed. Like his voice, and his face, and their memories together, some of what he'd taught her about the truck had faded. If he'd been there with them, he'd know exactly what to do. She squeezed her eyes shut in anguish, missing him more than ever.

Scott took his phone from his pocket and shone the flashlight feature into the shadows of the wheel well before he looked up and over his shoulder at Jack. "When was the last time you had—"

Jack gasped, stepping back toward the road, her mouth agape and her eyes wide. "Did you see that?"

Scott stood and grabbed her hand, pulling her away from the road. "Careful."

"What?" Fox stood and turned to face the trees, some so tall on either side of the road, they could only see a small slice of the sky above them. They were surrounded, closed in, and panic grew at an alarming rate in Fox's chest. "What did you see?"

Jack grabbed Scott's arm, her gaze transfixed on the trees in front of the truck. "I ... I saw something moving in there."

Chills scurried down her back, over and over, as she searched for a white skull mask through the trees, joining Jack's other side.

Jack pointed to a spot in the trees just up ahead from where they'd parked. "I thought I saw those bushes rustling, more than just the wind."

"There could be animals out here," Scott said, resting his hand on her mid back. "You should both get back in the truck."

The possibility of an animal watching them hadn't even occurred to Fox. Jack nodded and stepped toward the front of the truck.

Fox followed. "Can you fix it, Scott?"

Scott glanced back at the wheel. "If it's what I think, yes, but not here."

He hopped on the side runner and grabbed his axe from the truck bed, scanning the tree line again.

Jack passed the driver's side door. "What are our options?"

"Call a tow?" Fox asked, and reached out for Jack's hand, pulling her back toward the door.

We need to get in on this side, away from anything lurking in the woods.

"Let's discuss it in the truck." Scott opened the driver's side door, gripping the handle of the axe with his other hand.

"I have CAA." Jack stopped and turned back to them. "Remember, my parents gifted me my membership when you loaned me the truck?"

Fox nodded and ushered her into the truck. "Right, okay, let's call Costa for a ride, and we'll call to get it towed somewhere they can work on it for you in the morning."

Jack bit her lip, nodding slowly before scooting across the seat. "I have to drive back tomorrow. I have to be back before my class at one. I've got an exam. I guess I could call someone from school..."

Fox hoped she hadn't even considered calling Cooper for help.

Scott opened the door wider for Fox, staring down the road they came from before turning to them again. "I could just go back to that gas station and see if they have the tools I need. I could fix it for you."

"What?" Fox scoffed. "Walk back on your own? No way."

"We'd come with you," Jack said.

"I wouldn't leave you on your own—" Scott started.

"No." Fox turned to her as she pulled herself up into the truck. "No one should walk. We should call Costa for a ride and get it towed."

"We'll be alone here in the dark until the service gets here," Jack said. "And they might not even have time for me tomorrow at the shop."

"All the more reason we should call them now." Fox shivered, glancing past Jack at the trees through the window on the other side of the truck.

She scanned along the tree line, bracing herself to catch sight of a white mask emerging from the dark green pines, cedars, and the other trees that lost all their leaves.

"If you have to get back early"—Scott hopped into the truck—"I don't want you to have to wait when I'm perfectly capable of fixing it. I can do it early tomorrow morning back at my place. Lock up!"

Fox locked her door and rolled her window all the way up as he did the same.

"I can't miss this exam." Jack rubbed her temples with her fingers and turned to Fox. "This is bad. Can we have it towed to Scott's?"

Fox nodded and tapped the business number on Jack's card into her phone. She pressed it to her ear and mouthed "sure that's okay?" to Scott.

Scott nodded to Fox, leaning his axe against the floor of the truck and the seat between himself and Jack. "It would be my pleasure."

"I appreciate that." Jack leaned her head against him. "You're very sweet, you know that?"

What is he trying to do with that axe out here, anyway? Scott wants to be the hero with Jack in his presence—which is sweet—but I'm not about to walk around in the dark back to the gas station with a killer on the loose to find out if he's got a good swing.

As the phone rang, she kept her eyes on the tree line, watching for movement, waiting for the next bad thing to happen.

20

The mix of smoky cedar and stringent pine filled his nose before he donned his mask, stepping between the trees. He lifted his hood to hide himself enough to remain unseen until the time was right.

He'd caught the way the edge of the axe glinted in the moonlight as Scott removed it from the truck bed. What did he think he was going to do with that?

Fox came in and out of view as the tree branches swayed in the wind, her phone pressed to her ear. They'd almost caught him when the wind had shifted, revealing his hiding place. He'd retreated further into the trees and used the cover to shift closer to the truck. They'd almost confirmed the danger they must have been sensing, but they hadn't pursued him, and he had a theory as to why.

There were dark things in the world, things so terrible that most people would rather turn away than face what they feared most. They feared the things they didn't understand how to deal with or live with, and when it came down to taking action, they'd rather withdraw. His theory was born in part by survival instincts, psychological insight, and experience.

He twisted the bloody rope in the front pocket of his hoodie, the sticky blood drying up by the minute, coating his gloves. He'd made the mayor's mistress use it to tie him to a chair before he'd shoved her down on the opposite one. He'd held the knife in his back pocket to the mayor's throat and told her if she tried to run, he'd slit it. He'd banked on her staying put from the months of carefully gathered intelligence on her, after becoming the new accountant for her retail shop in town. Her expensive financial investments in her lover —the adulterer—gave him a good gauge of her emotional ones. If the new watch, new suit, and a trip to Windsor planned for the coming winter were any indication, she wouldn't move as long as she believed they'd make it out alive.

He'd been right.

She sat there as he stood behind the mayor, a knife to his throat. He produced his handgun, keeping it trained on her until he could reach her. The knife slid into her with ease. As she bled, losing her life before their eyes, the mayor begged, and shrieked, and tried to bargain with him until his mistress took her last breath on her basement carpet. He finished off the mayor shortly after with three stabs to his stomach in quick succession.

The mayor paid the toll twice, as he took the life of the one the mayor loved most, and then lost his own, just like they all would.

As he tightened his grip on the sticky, bloody rope, the pine tree branches swayed above him. His pulse raced. He took another step forward until all three were in sight in the cab of the truck.

He couldn't hear them—not yet. He had to get closer. He had to risk being seen, and even though it wasn't the right time—he trusted his gut on that—it *would* terrify them. And that would please him.

Once the mistress was dead, he'd told the mayor why they had to pay with their lives. He explained everything to him, so as he took his last breaths, he'd know the cost of the breath he'd stolen.

Another car approached, maintaining speed even as it merged into the oncoming lane to clear their truck.

The redhead could sense him—a product of his close proximity to her so many times when she didn't realize it. She'd had the most opportunity to step up, to warn others, and yet, she'd always retreated. She lacked conviction, which hadn't surprised him.

He had a plan—he always had multiple back-ups, because experience was a messy but invaluable teacher. Even if they caught him right then and there, he'd have the upper hand.

But the brown-haired one wouldn't look closer, and she wouldn't take the redhead seriously, despite her love for her cousin.

And the boy was too enamoured with her to see anything else at all.

In the end, they'd all wish they'd done something different—they had that in common.

Yes, he'd make them wish they'd done something different.

They'd pay the toll, twice.

This time—with the mayor and the mistress—hadn't been as good as the time before, and he knew why. They should have been spaced apart to make the suffering last, like he'd originally planned—but plans changed. He'd taken too great a risk. He'd cut it too close for comfort. If he failed at any point, the rest of them would go on with their lives, turning a blind eye to the dangers of the world, the damage they'd caused, and the darkness inside themselves.

Yes, he'd manage without the prolonged suffering if it meant they still paid the toll twice.

Three more to go.

21

Fox ended the call and studied the gaps between the trees by her window, waiting for movement. "We got lucky. They're close by. They should be here in ten."

"Wow. Okay." Jack sat up from where she'd laid her head on Scott's shoulder and rubbed her neck. "That's not bad at all."

Frustration welled up in Fox's chest, and she clenched her jaw as she tapped her phone screen.

Why didn't either of them call our friends for a ride while I ordered the tow? Is Jack really that drunk? I bet Scott was too preoccupied with being her hero, and turned on by the fact that she'd rested her head on his shoulder. Or maybe they were both too busy finding comfort in each other on the dark, isolated road to think ahead. Regardless, if our ride doesn't show up in fifteen minutes, we'll be out here, alone.

Fox sighed. "I'm calling Costa."

A rustling of branches in the trees made all three of them turn, but a squirrel bounded from branch to branch above. Headlights filled the cab as a car passed in the opposite direction of town, slowing down to check them out before speeding up around the next bend.

"I'm getting cold." Jack wrapped her arms across her chest.

Fox grabbed her coat and handed it to her, catching Scott's arm lifting from the corner of her eye, as if to wrap it around her. Headlights lit up the cab again, reflecting off the rear-view mirror. Scott stretched his arm out in front of him in a casual manner, Jack none the wiser as she pulled her coat on.

An old, black Cadillac, driving in the direction of town, slowed down as it approached. Fox frowned, squinting at it.

It passed, but as it did, Fox recognized Dylan in the driver's seat of the same car he'd used to pick her up and take her on their adventures. He squinted through the window at her as he passed. The car slowed down and parked on the gravel shoulder of the road just ahead.

"Dylan," Fox muttered, as they stared out the front windshield.

What were the odds?

"Are you kidding me?" Jack scoffed. "Just ignore him. He had no problem doing it to you."

Her terse quip in front of Scott irked Fox. She put it down to the alcohol, and the bitter taste in Jack's mouth from her own situation after the breakup with Cooper.

Dylan climbed out of the car and left his door ajar, walking toward them.

"What is he doing?" Jack hissed.

Out of all the roads and all the people in Auburn

Hills, it had to be him. Dylan stopped between his car and her truck. Scott opened his door.

"Everybody okay?" Dylan called.

"Yeah, we have a tow coming." Scott stepped out of the truck and walked alongside the hood as Dylan approached. "We're fine. Thanks, anyway!"

Dylan stopped and turned to Fox, nodding to her. "You need a ride?"

Fox wanted to say no. She wanted to tell him to leave. After the eerie connection the news had made between Piper Cornell and Crescent Moon Studios, it was such a weird coincidence that another part of that puzzle would show up—so weird that maybe it hadn't been a coincidence. *Did he follow us?*

Jack turned to her and shook her head, whispering, "Just call Costa and ignore this jerk."

"We've got a friend coming," Scott called back.

Headlights filled the cab of the truck from behind them as a tow truck drove around the corner, slowing down as it approached.

"Wow, that was fast," Jack muttered, sitting up straighter.

The driver leaned forward, checking out the space between Dylan's car and their truck—possibly trying to gauge if he had enough room between them. Dylan stood there watching her. Was he waiting to hear it from her? Did he want to make sure she was okay? She hated that she enjoyed the thought.

Scott rejoined them at his open window and leaned in. "Wanna make a call?"

If it wasn't a coincidence, she wanted to know why,

and if it was, she had her own questions to ask him, anyway.

Fox turned to Jack. "Costa's going to take another fifteen to twenty minutes to get here and then fifteen to get back. We could just get back in fifteen and enjoy the rest of our night."

"Seriously?" Jack cocked her head to the side and stared at her.

Scott waved to the tow truck driver and turned to Jack. "She's got a point. I don't like the idea of standing around, waiting for a ride on this road. Let's just get out of here."

The tow truck honked, presumably at Dylan to move his car, but he continued looking at Fox.

"Ugh, fine," Jack moaned.

Fox nodded once to Dylan, and a hint of a smile formed on his lips as he squinted against the headlights of the tow truck.

"Will you get your car out of the way?" Jack shouted, waving him off.

He turned on his heel and strode back to his car, sliding in.

"I can't believe this," Jack muttered, grabbing her purse and the tray of slushies. "Of all the people to come along, Cooper's the only one I can think of that would have been worse."

"Then it's a good thing he's hours away." Fox gathered her work bag and the bags of treats, then opened her door.

Scott reached in and pulled the key from the ignition.

Jack released a deep sigh. "I can't believe you're agreeing to this after he ghosted you."

Fox hauled the bags out of the truck, ignoring the comment, and hopped onto the gravel.

Jack followed and rounded the hood, joining Scott's side as they approached the tow truck. Scott handed the driver the keys through the window, and he handed Scott a clipboard as Fox passed them. She walked along the gravel shoulder toward the passenger's side of Dylan's car, her chest tight at the thought of getting into that passenger seat again where they'd shared so many good times.

Dylan hopped out and hustled around to the other side with a speed she hadn't seen him provide for the tow truck. He opened the door for her, as he always had.

"Thanks," she muttered, stepping in.

He shut the door for her. The familiar scent of eucalyptus reminded her of the hand lotion he'd kept in the glove compartment. He hustled around the front again and sat beside her, closing his door and leaning back against his seat. He stared forward, rubbing his hand over his mouth.

"Where were you going?" Fox asked. "And where's Tinker Bell?"

"I just dropped her off at our parents' for the night." *So, she's his sister. Why do I even care who he was with?* She had no reasonable explanation for it. "I was on my way home, back to Toronto. Where can I take you?"

Home.

She wanted to say it, but the more time that passed since she saw that red "Sold" sign, the less genuine the word felt. She kept her jaw clenched, resting the bags between her feet.

"Your aunt and uncle's?" he asked. "You still staying there?"

"How did you know that?" She looked over at him for the first time, trying to catch his gaze as the realization settled in.

She'd been living in her own apartment the whole time they'd known each other. He'd quit the studio before it closed down, and she'd moved in with her aunt and uncle after that.

Jack and Scott opened the back doors and slid in.

He shifted into drive, leaning in closer. "I just wanted to make sure you were okay."

"You followed me?" she whispered.

He cleared his throat. "Hawkstone Drive?"

Fox nodded, folding her arms over her chest as she turned to the back seat. Jack gave her an expression that seemed to suggest they'd made a mistake. Jack glanced at Dylan, held up two fingers, jabbed them in the direction of her eyes, and then toward the back of his headrest. Something in Fox's eyes must have told Jack she shared the sentiment.

22

As they pulled up beside the large, white sign on the boulevard, Dylan parked along the curb beside it. Ryan's van sat parked in the driveway behind Costa's empty car.

As soon as the car stopped, Jack clicked her seatbelt off. "Thank you."

She pushed the door open and stepped out quickly, carrying her tray of melted slushies with her.

"Thanks!" Scott called, getting out, and they closed their doors at the same time.

"We appreciate the ride." Fox unclicked her seatbelt, and as it retracted, Jack stopped by the curb beside her, her arms crossed, waiting. "Thanks for helping us out."

"I didn't do it for you." Dylan stared ahead. "I did it for me."

Fox hesitated with her fingertips on the handle. Jack's shadow from the streetlight swayed side to side along the dashboard. Fox appreciated her presence as Dylan turned to her.

"I wanted to spend time with you," his low, confident voice demanded her attention, but she stared at the handle on her door, both hating and wanting his words at the same time. She'd waited too long for an explanation after he left, and then the studio went under, and she'd resigned herself to the fact that she'd never see him again and that it was obviously for the best. But there he was, speaking the words she'd longed to hear while they were together. "It's so weird that I saw you tonight after what they're running on the news—"

"Let's go!" Jack called.

Fox made eye contact with her as Scott turned around before reaching the driveway, realizing Jack wasn't moving until Fox came with them. He joined Jack's side. Fox nodded to them, holding up a finger.

She turned back to Dylan, the hollows of his cheeks dark in the shadows of the car. "You saw the studio on the news. What happened? Where did you go, and why did they just randomly shut down?"

"I'm sorry," Dylan said, not in a rush, or a mumble. Just a clean and clear apology. "I'm not proud of the way things ended, how I stopped answering you. You didn't deserve that, and I think that's why I stopped in the first place. We were getting too close..."

It was all excuses to make himself feel like he'd done her a favour by randomly seeming to cease to exist one day of his choosing.

Fox turned to him suddenly. "Did you know Piper Cornell?"

His chest heaved, and he swallowed audibly, his gaze

falling to the console between them as he ran his fingers through his hair.

"You did, didn't you?"

He nodded yes. "She started a little after I did. I did shoots with her, but I never knew who she was. I just found out. You were all numbers to me—the ones you'd been assigned. It's what I was told to call you all—"

"I know that. We've been over this. Did you know her well?"

"Just at work."

She scoffed. "Well, we started just at work, too, and you can be pretty flirty with your co-workers, so forgive me for asking—"

"That's fair, but the insinuation isn't. What you and I had was different." He licked his lips and swallowed hard again, shaking his head. "I never spoke to any of the others outside of work, and I only had contact with one of the owners. I only ever saw him in person once, when he hired me. It was odd from the beginning that way, but I started getting the feeling something wasn't right when they'd delay my pay by a week, and then two weeks. They got so behind, and they'd never give me any answers. I figured they were pocketing my share for themselves when you told me there wasn't anything weird going on with your pay. I quit because I thought they were stiffing me, but then I got this letter delivered to my home. They said they knew I'd broken the contract by meeting up with you outside of work, and that if I gave them any trouble in the future, or continued to see you, they'd take legal action against me for the violation. It was total bullshit—they're the ones who shorted me.

They said it was for your safety—or the safety of their employees—I don't remember. The letter made them look like professionals, like the good guys—"

"So, you just stopped talking to me? You couldn't even give me a reason why?"

"I told you that last time we spoke on the phone. I said you should leave the studio because you could do something so much greater with your life. I tried to warn you—"

"That was a warning?" She sneered. "Well, Dylan, thanks so much for my warning—"

"I'm sorry, Fox. There's no good excuse."

She pulled the handle and pushed the car door open, hesitating as the interior light lifted the heavy, secretive mood. She needed to know more—anything he knew about Piper's murder. "When was the last time you spoke with Piper?"

"I don't know. Like I said, I never knew who she was. Why are you asking about Piper? Did you become friends?"

She shook her head no. "I never knew her. I didn't know any of them like—"

Like she knew him, until she realized she hadn't known him at all.

"Ready?" Jack called.

Scott took the tray from Jack's hands and took a step back onto the front lawn. Jack followed his lead, giving Fox more space and privacy.

Dylan rubbed his fingers against the wheel. "Listen, I don't know anything about Piper. I'm sorry."

Was the bride from the basement right? Was Slate

Cornell driven to violence? Did he check into that facility, not seeing an end to the pain in sight, then check out with a plan? The witness to his daughter's murder. The people in the basement after that. What did they have to do with his daughter? What would his motive be? What would be his end game?

"How many other girls worked for the studio?" she asked.

"Twenty, maybe? Thirty, max. They kept it small."

"Do you think her dad knew?" *And was one of those stabbing victims in the basement one of those girls? And one of the brothers—one of the owners of Crescent Moon Studio?*

He shook his head. "I can only assume she was respectful of the contract. She probably followed the rules, *just like you.*"

What is he trying to say? His sarcasm rubbed her the wrong way. She avoided eye contact and gathered the bags from between her feet.

"Does she know?" He nodded to Jack. "That's your cousin, Jack, isn't it? She's protective of you, so she knows, right?"

Fox took a deep breath and whispered, "Yes."

"Good." He pressed his lips together, nodding as he scanned the dark street ahead.

She frowned. "Why would you say that?"

"Because it's a risk you take, and if no one knows you're there..."

"Did this happen to Piper because of the studio? The brothers? Was someone there involved?"

"I'm not saying that at all. I'm saying... I don't know what I'm saying. Just... just take care of yourself, okay?

And just because they shut down that operation doesn't mean they aren't still around. Who knows..."

"That's why you didn't contact me, even after they closed. You think they're doing the same thing with others..."

"And cheating more people out of money." He scratched his head at the back of his neck. "And think about it, okay. I didn't tell anyone in my personal life what kind of photography I was doing, but you did. Maybe Piper did, too."

But why would anyone have killed her because of it?

Dylan ran his hand around the steering wheel once, then reversed the other way like he used to when he was about to share something with her. "I was in town, visiting family this summer. I stopped by your old apartment, and when you weren't there, your neighbour told me where you'd moved. I wasn't following you. I was trying to reconnect."

But he hadn't.

"You went to the trouble of finding out where I moved to. If you were trying to see me again, what stopped you?"

He pressed his lips together, his chest heaving, leaving them in silence.

"The studio? You thought we were still in violation of the contract? Come on, Dylan. No. You came to my apartment. You were ready to see me. You can't blame the studio for everything. Maybe... maybe the studio isn't connected to these deaths at all." She huffed, shaking her head as she stepped out of the car.

"The killer wears a mask, doesn't he?" he said in a

low tone. She ducked her head back in. "So did we. Think that's a coincidence?"

"I don't know," she muttered, the hairs on her arm standing on end as she lingered in the open doorway. All the things she hadn't been sure of piled up within her, and as she uttered the words, she was sure she'd fall apart unless she got some answers. "Were you following us tonight?"

He frowned. "What? No."

Maybe Dylan was like Scott. He'd wanted to show up and be the hero, but all he'd done was make excuses, expect her to read his mind about his subliminal warning message, and make suggestions about their involvement in whatever the hell was going on with The Skull Masked Murderer. Nothing Piper had done at the studio could have warranted her murder. Until Fox discovered the identities of the bodies murdered in the basement, she couldn't be sure there were any more connections to Crescent Moon. Maybe Jack was right—maybe she'd read too much into it.

"If you think the fact that we wore masks... that we did what we did..." She leaned in further, her voice shaking. "I haven't done anything wrong, and I never did anything I thought would hurt somebody. I can go to sleep at night with the choices I make."

She stood and shut the door, carrying the bags to Jack and Scott on the front lawn. The three of them watched as Dylan drove away, leaving her more confused and unsettled than the first time he left.

Jack took one of the bags for her. "What did he—"

A shrill scream echoed from somewhere behind them, and they turned in unison.

Jack gasped. "Was that the backyard?"

Scott turned back to them, wide-eyed.

Fox bolted down the dark side of the house.

23

The dark tree line ahead bounced before Fox's eyes as she jogged to the backyard.

"Hey, wait," Scott called. "Jack!"

As she rounded the corner, Kerry stood laughing beside the hot tub in her Buffy outfit splattered with wet spots, her stake nowhere to be seen. She dug her palm into the water and splashed Ryan in the hot tub.

"Easy, Cordelia. He'll get you." Costa pulled his shirt off, shaking his head at them with a grin. "I didn't think I'd be going in the hot tub tonight, so I'm goin' in my boxers!"

"Hey," Kerry called to them as Fox caught her breath and Jack stopped at her side.

Cordelia—not Buffy. Why hadn't I considered that?

It had been Kerry's sharp scream.

"What took you guys so long?" Ryan leaned back as water bubbles surrounded his chest, resting his hands behind his head. "You ready to strip?"

A lump rose in Fox's throat as flashbacks of her

photoshoots filled her thoughts. Instead of retreating, she tried to focus on the faces of the other girls. She'd seen Piper Cornell's photo on the news, but she hadn't recognized her. Not her hair, or her skin, or her lips.

Kerry's smile faded as she glanced from Fox to Jack and back. "Sorry. Maybe we shouldn't have turned it on and opened it before you got here. The house was locked, so we were just hanging out back here—"

"No." Jack waved her off, pulling her key out of her purse. "You guys are fine. You got this party started. I'll unlock the house and bring some snacks out to the table."

"I can help!" Kerry called.

"No, it's fine," Jack called over her shoulder.

"Booze is by the back door, ready to be put on ice," Ryan called to her, slurring as Jack rounded the side of the house, disappearing into the darkness. "Bring me two more G and Ts, will ya? C'mon in, Angel, the water's warm."

"I told you"—Costa laughed, tossing his shirt aside —"I'm not Angel."

"My Doyle's looking *hot tonight!*" Kerry shouted as Costa stepped into the hot tub, a devilish grin on his lips as he watched her.

Fox went to follow Jack, stepping toward the side of the house, eager to get out of her combination of work uniform and costume, and into comfy clothes.

Scott stepped out of the shadows. "Fox?"

She stopped, pressing her hand to her chest.

"Sorry. Can I get your advice on something?"

"Sure, let's walk and talk." She turned, but he put his hand on her arm, stopping her. "What's up? You okay?"

He glanced over his shoulder and then hers. "I'm concerned about Jack, and... could you keep something just between us? I know that's a big ask because you tell her everything, but... I'd rather her not know I told you."

She rested her hands on her hips, frowning. "I'm not going to keep anything from her, but if there's something serious going on, you need to tell me."

Scott looked past her, and she checked over her shoulder. Jack had already rounded the front corner of the house. She couldn't stand any more secrets—especially not Jack's.

"I won't tell her *you* told me, if that's what you want?"

"Okay." Scott sighed. "Just before we left the party, when you came out front and saw Jack and me? I found her there, on her phone, talking to her ex."

"Okay..."

He wrung his hands and took a step closer. "It was on speakerphone, and he told her he's coming here. Tonight."

"Here?" She raised her voice, and he rested his hand on her shoulder, widening his eyes. "Sorry."

"She told him not to—screamed it, actually. Then, she hung up on him. I just wanted to warn you that he might be trying to come here and start something."

She shook her head and walked past him toward the side of the house. "He's not welcome here. I won't let him in."

"I wouldn't, either." Scott followed. "But do we really have a choice?"

She stopped and frowned, expecting him to have put up more of a fight. "What do you mean? Of course we do. It's Jack's parents' house—"

"She took his call, Fox. She might have even been the one to call him. I don't know if she's over him yet."

"She's the one who broke up with him. She wouldn't have called him, and you heard it yourself. She doesn't want him here."

"Well, we're here, and we'd make sure nothing happened." He nodded to himself.

That was the Scott she knew, calm and collected, but not totally confident like he portrayed himself to be around Jack.

She started toward the front of the house. "She doesn't need this."

"She doesn't deserve this." Scott stopped at the front door and lowered his voice. "Fox, could you level with me here? Do you think I have a shot with Jack?"

"It's, umm... she just got out of this relationship, and she lives almost three hours away." *Which means if Cooper really left as soon as he threatened to, he could be here soon. Maybe Jack didn't take him seriously, and that's why she didn't share it with me. Or maybe it's because we've had no real time alone together for her to share it. Maybe Jack didn't believe Cooper would actually come all this way.* "I don't know if you'd consider that a long-distance relationship, but..."

"Has she ever said anything about me?" Scott asked.

"It's been almost a year since I met her. Has she ever mentioned if she's attracted to me, or..."

She heard her own voice instead of Scott's, the voice in her head asking the same questions about Dylan last year. They'd hung out together, but like Jack, he'd given her no real reason to believe they'd ever be anything more than friends. She'd wanted more for herself, and she wanted more for Scott.

Fox lowered her voice and took a step closer to him. "Let me put it to you this way. She's been too busy with that douche to notice anybody else, but I think since she's been back, she's noticed you."

The light from the lantern beside the door reflected in his eyes as his face lit up. He practically glowed as Fox opened the door and stepped inside. Scott followed, closing it and locking it behind them. They walked down the hallway, toward the kitchen.

"I'm not trying to rush anything, but I'm wondering if I have a chance, you know?" Scott asked in a hushed tone. "You're her cousin. Her best friend. You know her better than anyone, so if anyone could tell me if I actually have a shot, it's you."

They stopped at the kitchen counter, facing the backyard. Out the window, Jack pulled her towel off, revealing one of her red bikinis. She grabbed a can of beer before joining the others in the hot tub.

Fox set her bag on the back counter. "Let me put it to you this way. If you did, in fact, have a shot at something with my cousin, you just risked upsetting her and ruining it for yourself in order to tell me about someone who could hurt her—

someone I want to protect her from. I don't have a say in whether or not she likes you, Scott, but after these last two days, I think you're the kind of guy I'd like to see her with."

He smiled, looking back at Jack in the hot tub. "Thanks, Fox."

"I'll meet you guys out there, okay?" Fox nodded to the hot tub and handed him the outdoor speaker. He took it, but she didn't let go. "For the record, whether either of us think you have a shot or not, it'd be a shame not to try. You don't want to have to ask yourself 'what if?'"

He sighed as she released the speaker, remaining frozen in place and deep in thought.

Fox left him, walking down the hallway to the foyer and up the stairs to her room. "If she asks, I'm changing into my bathing suit, and I'll be out in a sec!"

Fox pulled the no-longer-matching necklace off, then tugged the turtleneck over her head, leaving their matching ones on as she always had while slipping out of the rest of her clothes. She opened the closet in a fog, pulled her one-piece bathing suit from a hanger, and stepped into it, pulling the straps over her arms as she stared into the closet.

It all had to be packed in a week. The last twenty-four hours felt surreal.

Her gaze lingered on the edge of the black mask with little wings carved into the sides that sat on her shelf in the closet.

They all wore masks...

She grabbed a towel hanging from the back of her door in a daze and hesitated, her laptop in sight. She walked back to Jack's desk, grabbed it, and sat on the bed, opening it on her lap.

She'd searched the name Piper Cornell a few times after her murder last month. The first matches on the list were news articles, YouTube videos, and video clips from the local news that had been made about her murder. There'd been nothing about Crescent Moon Studios then. She searched Piper's name again and scrolled further down, stopping at a bold headline with both familiar names: *Slate Cornell, Father of Slain Piper, Wanted for Questioning in Disappearance of Witness and the Brutal Stabbings of Two People Revealed to be William Bonetti, Auburn Hills' Mayor, and a Local Businesswoman.*

She gripped the sides of the screen, reading the headline again.

The mayor? Had he known about Crescent Moon Studios? Was he a silent partner, or did he back it financially, or maybe he had some other involvement that would warrant a motive for murder? Or were their deaths unrelated?

She searched just the business name, Crescent Moon Studios. Her own appeared among four others: Piper Cornell, Laura Thompson, Nicole Epps, and Victoria Castle. Her heart raced as she hovered the arrow over the article, afraid to click on it. They had her identity. *Do they have photos of my body, too?* She could barely breathe, clutching the sides of her laptop again.

It was all over—they were all going to know.

These girls would be discovering the same thing if they hadn't already, and if they'd found them, they'd find the rest eventually. Twenty or thirty like Dylan said? Who were they?

The eerie feeling returned, the one that hadn't truly left since the previous night when someone chased her around the building at work. It was more than a fear about being exposed. It pushed her to release her grip on the laptop and forced her to type.

Piper Cornell's name drew headlines from national news outlets. Fox had seen Piper's face, along with her father's, plastered on the local newspaper all month long. She squinted at her, trying to remember which girl she might have been, and which jobs she worked with her. Slate's arm was wrapped around her in one picture, with another around his short, blonde wife who'd passed away of cancer three years before.

Slate was alone in the world, and with nothing left to lose, she could see how he could become reckless, seeking justice for what happened to his daughter. But why go after the witness and the mayor, not to mention the mayor's side piece?

Laura Thompson's name search hadn't even returned a page worth of information relevant to her. From her social media, she seemed like a professional ballet dancer living in Toronto. That would have been a bit of a commute north for her to the studio. No distinguishing marks on her face or body to jog Fox's memory of her.

Nicole Epps's social media accounts came up first, too. The pixie cut and small, pouty lips stood out as memorable features. Fox knew her. There'd only been one woman that she'd seen with a pixie cut while modelling at the studio. Yes, that had to be her. She couldn't find anything else on her except her social accounts, where she mostly posted pictures with what looked like friends and family, seeming to reside in Auburn Hills.

Victoria Castle's name garnered plenty of results.

The first news article headline from the prior year read *Two Crash. One Dead on Halloween Night in Auburn Hills.*

The picture beside it was a black car, crashed into a tree on a downward angle. She scrolled down, scanning the article. *Paramedics responded to the scene, discovering the body of Victoria Castle and her father, John Castle, who was rushed to the Auburn Hills Hospital to receive care for minor injuries. John Castle was driving at the time of the accident, and upon impact with a tree in the ditch on Black Creek Road, his daughter was thrown from the car through the windshield, down the hill, and into Black Creek Park and conservation area in the early evening hours this Halloween—*

The second picture caught her eye, pulling her away from the writing. It was a close-up portrait of a young girl about her age, with medium, shoulder-length brown hair. Her round face; big, doe-shaped green eyes; and soft features juxtaposed with her black-and-white tattoos. Small stars were speckled along the side of her neck, trailing beneath the V-neck collar of her shirt.

That *was Victoria?* She recognized those tattoos from some of her first shoots. She was there for the pool party with tropical fruit. She also had a black bird with spread wings on her back shoulder blade, and a flower—some kind of flower—on her ankle. *Victoria's dead?*

Her chest ached as she clicked on the link to her obituary and scanned through it.

Daughter of the late Sadie Castle.

Survived by father, John Castle.

Both John Castle and Slate Cornell lost their daughters—Castle last Halloween, and Cornell last month. *Were the murders a result of something happening between those fathers, isolated to their families? Was the crash really an accident? Or was someone coming after those associated with Crescent Moon Studios?*

Her body answered for her as she settled into her truth.

She'd felt it at work.

She'd felt it at the party.

Someone was after her. If it was related, would their safety be jeopardized with their names exposed, or did the killer already know who they were?

If The Skull Masked Murderer was coming for her, and the other women too, she needed to tell Jack, and she needed to figure out why.

24

Laughter echoed from the basement as Fox walked down the hallway, past the open door. Some of them must have been playing pool. For comfort, she pulled one of her dad's oversized band T-shirts over her head. She walked straight to the back door, her heart racing. She needed to tell Jack that her secret was out. She needed to work everything through with her and figure out what the hell was happening.

She opened the back door and started to step outside, then stopped.

Jack and Scott grinned at each other in the corner of the hot tub, inching their faces closer together. Jack's lips parted as she closed her eyes. Fox's hand remained on the knob as she froze, anxiously caught in their private moment while acoustic rock played on the outdoor speaker.

Scott's hand emerged from the bubbling water, and he held her chin in his wet, dripping fingers, speaking so softly Fox couldn't hear what he said. Jack opened her eyes, and the soft, sensual smile she'd had melted away into confusion.

"I respect you too much to do something like this while you're so vulnerable."

Pain appeared in her glassy eyes as she pressed her lips together. Would Scott recognize that pain like Fox— as her best friend and closest confidant—could?

"Don't get me wrong." His arm disappeared into the water again, seeming to touch her leg. "I *want* to kiss you."

Jack smiled, her hazy gaze focusing back on him. "Yeah?"

"I've wanted to ever since the first day I saw you, and... it shocked me." He licked his lips and lowered his voice, his words more muffled by the bubbling waters and chorus of the song. "You—you have this way about you... and I've been ... since."

"I had no idea," Jack said.

Fox read her lips.

Scott laughed and held her hand as their grip floated atop the bubbles. "Well, I'm not the most forward. You've been drinking, and you're just getting out of something, and this isn't how I want it to go. Not for you. Not for us."

Jack nodded, her stare fluttering from him to the water, then back to him. She was definitely still drunk, even after their sobering almost-accident on the way back. In the past, Jack had tried to reassure Fox whenever she'd brought up a fear or concern, but right now Fox worried Jack wasn't in the right mind to discuss her issues. A hollowness developed inside her—feeling more alone than ever—questioning if she should even bring it up to her.

"Jack, if you feel the same in the morning, I'll be here. If you don't, I'll still be here to help you with your truck, and you can head back home knowing I care about you. I just want to see you happy, okay?"

Jack nodded, smiling, and threw her arms around his neck. She pulled him in for a tight hug, blinking rapidly as she finally noticed Fox standing in the open doorway.

"Hey!" Jack called. She pulled herself away from Scott, and they both turned to her. "There you are."

"Sorry to interrupt," Fox called, contemplating leaving them outside to enjoy their time together while she tormented herself alone, locked in her bedroom. But she'd wanted Jack to tell her the truth about her life, and she had to do the same. No secrets and no lies. And she needed her more than ever. "Jack, can we talk for a sec?"

Jack stood and stepped toward the side, sliding on the slick surface. Scott grabbed her by the waist, steadying her as they both laughed. He stepped out of the hot tub first and held her hand, supporting her as she climbed out more gracefully than Fox had expected. Maybe it was selfish to hope she'd sober up and be able to offer the support she so desperately yearned for—the presence Jack had been promising and failing to deliver. Maybe they really were Ginger and Brigitte, after all.

Scott wrapped a towel around Jack, and she scurried to meet Fox at the door. Scott picked up his own towel.

"They're in the basement, playing pool I think," Fox called to Scott, and he nodded to her before she closed the door behind them.

Fox led Jack past the kitchen and down the hallway as Ryan's cackling laughter echoed up the stairs.

"You'll never guess what just happened!" Jack whispered with glee.

Scott opened the back door and stepped inside as they turned left for the staircase, catching a glimpse of him shirtless. Jack giggled, turning over her shoulder to look at him.

Through the thin, long windowpane beside the front door, a beam of light appeared. It shone through as Fox stepped in front of it, squinting at the brown car driving down the street toward the house. *Elisha's boyfriend. Great.*

"Hey, Scott," Fox called, grabbing Jack's hand as she turned back to him. "I guess Elisha and her boyfriend changed their minds. They're here. Could you let them in?"

Before he could answer, Fox pushed Jack in front of her and marched her upstairs.

"Didn't see that coming," Jack whispered, breaking out into a giggling fit. "Mr. Pumpkin Head seemed grumpy as hell and bored to death with us all."

Fox pulled her into their bedroom at the top of the stairs and shut the door behind them.

"Listen," she said, grabbing Jack's shoulders. "I have to tell you something, and I need you to listen. They know. The news found out about the studio, right? And they must have done more digging, because my name is out there. *My name.*"

"That's... that's a violation of privacy, isn't it? Don't they have journalistic integrity? Shouldn't they have tried to contact you before putting your name out there like that?" Jack clutched the towel at her chest and paced the short length of the bedroom. "But it was closed down, right? They closed down in the spring, right? How did they find you?"

"Jack, Piper Cornell modelled for the studio, too. The girl who was murdered last month. The media found out, and they're running stories on the studio, the people who ran it, and the women... They have some of our names. They must have a source..."

Jack pressed her hand to her mouth, her eyes wide in shock, shaking her head.

"I don't know what's happening." She held Jack's arms again. "One of the girls lives in the city. Another one lives here. Then, there was Piper—murdered. Then another girl who got in a car accident a little over a year ago—she *died*. They have our names, Jack, and they're running them."

"Shit," Jack spat, grabbing Fox's arms the way she'd just held Jack's. "What does this mean?"

"I don't know if the car accident was really an accident. I think... Piper's dad might have found out what she was doing, who she was working with. People might be coming after the girls. He might be out for revenge. Or —or maybe it was someone else involved with the studio..."

"Dylan?" Jack asked, patting herself dry with the towel.

His comment about the masks came to the forefront of Fox's mind, but she shook her head a second later. "Maybe, but I don't think so. Something else is going on.

Even the witness to her murder could have been involved somehow, and that's why he went missing. Maybe the mayor was involved—an investor in the company? Maybe the woman he was found with worked for the company, and... and..."

"The mayor?" Jack furrowed her brow.

"The couple stabbed to death in the basement today? That was the mayor and another woman that *wasn't* his wife."

Jack pressed her lips together, deep in thought, and hung the towel on the back of the door. "You think it's all connected?"

"I don't know." She ran both of her hands through her hair from her forehead to the crown of her head, tugging at it, desperate to relieve some of the pressure forming beneath. "Is it a coincidence that I was involved with the same company Piper worked with? Was that girl's car accident even an accident? Is there a cover-up going on, or is this... I don't know, revenge? If Slate Cornell just left the mental health facility, the timing... It can't all be a coincidence, can it? Now, he's wanted for questioning, but that could be a diversion, or a distraction... I've had this really bad feeling, Jack. I need you to hear me."

Jack wrapped her arms around Fox, squeezing her damp body against her front. In seconds, she received the presence from her she'd been wishing for. Fox held her close, releasing a shuddering sigh against her shoulder.

"Let's send everybody home," Jack's raspy voice came from beside her ear, maintaining her grip on Fox. "Let's just clear out the house, and then it'll just be us, and we can talk this through."

Fox nodded, sinking into her embrace. "Thank you. I'm—I'm spiralling here, Jack."

Jack pulled away from her. "No way. It's nothing we can't handle, you hear me? We'll get the authorities involved if we have to. I mean, terms and contracts *must* have been violated, right? You were supposed to remain anonymous, and now you feel like this is all connected somehow. Should we be calling the police?"

"I don't know... I think... I mean, my involvement with the studio was confidential right? Somehow, that..." Fox cleared her throat, swallowed hard, and whispered, "That was violated. I accepted the terms believing I'd remain anonymous..."

Jack strode to the door. "I knew there was a risk this could happen. I told you. You remember what else I said?"

She turned to Fox and waited.

"You told me to only take it if the risk was worth the reward. That money supported my independence. I knew it'd get me my own place, even just to rent, but it afforded me a bit of financial security. A bit of independence, even for a short time. At the time, it was worth it."

Jack rested her hand on the knob, nodding. "You accepted the risk, and I told you I'd be here if this ever happened."

"Everyone's going to find out what I was doing," Fox whispered. "And they're going to see... all of me. Our family—"

"Your mom will be supportive. She's a free spirit, and

she'll think it's liberating—despite the way this is all happening." Jack took a deep breath and hooked her index finger on her matching necklace, running it back and forth until she clutched the medallion. "I hate this for you."

"Your parents won't like it. They'd never approve of that. My dad, he would have been angry..."

Like Slate Cornell?

"I'm here. I'm standing in support of you. I think you're a total badass for using your assets to your advantage. It's your body, and you're proud of it." Jack grabbed a shirt from the closet, opened the door, and smiled. "And people are going to see it, but I mean, lucky them."

It was everything she needed to hear but it wouldn't make it go away. She knew it wouldn't. Her mind kept racing, finding the next worst thing.

"Everyone from work..." Fox whispered, thinking of the group downstairs, of Kennedy, as Jack walked to the top of the landing, pulling the oversized pink T-shirt over her head.

She was already losing her home, and if she lost her job, and the respect of her family, what would she have?

Jack turned to her at the staircase with a confident smile, her warm, brown eyes reassuring as ever. "We'll get through this, okay? You and me. We always do."

Jack. She'd have Jack, just like it always had been.

"We'll figure this Crescent Moon stuff out." Jack grabbed the banister. "We'll go over everything we know. I just have to see our friends out, okay?"

Suddenly, Fox felt naked with only her dad's shirt on over her swimsuit. She needed to change into clothes, or pajamas, or a big hoodie she'd claimed of her fathers before her mom sent a pile out for donation.

"I'll be down in a sec, okay?" Fox asked, somehow mustering a genuine smile. "Love you, Ethel."

"Love you, Lucy." Jack nodded and took a few steps down the stairs. Fox started to close the door to her room, but a cold draft stopped her as Jack hesitated on the stairs. She waited for her to turn around and say something more.

"Scott, what're you doing down there?" Jack asked, her amused tone remaining. "Why'd you leave the front door open like that?"

She hopped down another step, and another. "Scott, come on. That isn't funny. Did Ryan put you up to this?"

Fox opened her door again and stepped out into the hallway, walking to the top of the stairs as a sinking feeling pushed from her lungs down into her stomach.

Jack took another few steps, leaning over the railing for a better view of whatever the scene was below. Fox took the steps quickly, rushing to join her side as the dark night beyond the open front door came into view.

Jack grabbed the railing, releasing a shrill scream. "Scott!"

A pool of bright red blood bloomed beneath Scott's head in the hallway below.

25

Jack started down the steps, and Fox grabbed her hand, holding her back.

"What if it's not a prank?" Jack hissed.

"Then we need to call for help, but I don't have my phone up here. It's downstairs in my bag. And he has your phone, remember?" She nodded to Scott, where he lay awkwardly, his body sprawled across half the hallway.

"Fox..."

Fox shook her head no and whispered, "If it's not a prank, someone did that to him, and they could still be here. We have to get to my phone in the kitchen."

She took a step down, and Jack did the same, slowly, one by one until they reached the tile floor. They peered out the open door as the wind whistled beyond. Elisha's boyfriend's car sat parked along the curb by the "For Sale" sign where they'd been with Dylan.

The urge to bolt through the door crossed Fox's mind, dreams of reaching the neighbour's house forming as the cold tile beneath her feet shocked her back into the present moment, to the possible danger that lurked beyond the door, waiting just outside for them. Her body thrummed with adrenaline; her short, quick breaths designed to help her hear potential threats mimicked the feeling of a panic attack coming on.

"Fox," Jack whispered, fear filling her tone.

She had to keep her wits about her. She couldn't succumb to the dizzying feeling that whirled in her mind, churned at her stomach, and stole her breath.

Fox led them to the right and down the hallway. As they shuffled past Scott, Jack lingered, bending down toward him slowly. Fox steadied her as she braced herself for a scream, or a scare, or for Scott to pop up and laugh. He didn't move, and Jack's hand gripped Fox's as her other hand patted his side by his visible pocket.

"That's real blood," Jack hissed, turning back to her. "I'm almost sure of it, and no phone."

Fox's arm hairs stood on end as she pulled Jack past the closed basement door into the kitchen. Was that door open before? She scanned their surroundings, catching no sounds or movements, and bolted to the counter. Jack stood back to back with her as Fox grabbed her bag, rifling through it.

The phone was gone. Not lost. Gone.

The churning in her stomach stopped, and she clenched her muscles, more convinced than ever that danger was an arm's length away and they had no way to call for help.

"They took my phone," Fox whispered.

"Who?"

Fox turned to her. "Whoever did *that* to Scott. We have to go and get help. We're leaving. *Now*."

She pulled Jack along toward the back door. As she grabbed the knob, she noticed the hot tub bubbling bright red—almost pink—and seemingly empty from their vantage point. Jack gasped, pushing her hand to her mouth. It was an elaborate prank, if it was one, and if it was, they'd regret it. Fox would make sure of it. She led Jack back down the front hallway, and as they passed the basement door, a scream echoed from the other side.

Fox jumped as a thudding, banging sound on the stairs followed. They turned to each other before Jack held her arm out, ready to keep the door shut. They took turns stepping over Scott, stumbling toward the open front door as Fox's heart pounded in her ears in time with the footsteps. The basement door slammed open. A figure in the skull mask, splattered with blood, stepped up into the bright hallway. The tall figure rushed toward them, reaching out with blood on their hands. They groaned and moaned—the sounds so familiar, and a metallic smell mixed with chlorine wafted toward them.

Jack released a cry and pushed him away. He stumbled back with ease, tripping over Scott and falling to the hallway floor beside him, just a few feet away from the basement door. He pushed both bloody hands against his stomach, against the dark, shiny patch of material on his faded black hoodie, writhing in pain.

Was it a trick? A prank? No, it was real, and it was...

"Ryan?" Fox screamed.

It reverberated inside her—an alarm warning her

that *everything* was real, and wrong, and they needed to get out.

"Umph," the figure huffed, shaking his head and sputtering, "He ..."

Fox stepped forward, bending over Scott, and pulled the mask off. She revealed his messy, brown hair, his eyes squeezed shut. Ryan. He blinked, his gaze trailing up her bare legs, to her oversized shirt, to her eyes. The pain that filled his expression broke her, her legs about to buckle beneath her. He kept one hand on his stomach as the other reached out toward her arm.

Somehow, despite her internal warning bells and the inner knowing that had been proven by the irrefutable evidence before her, for one brief moment, Fox expected him to laugh or smile, or for Scott to get up. She offered him her hand, and he squeezed so tightly, she almost pulled away to stop the pain shooting through her.

"Run," Ryan sputtered, blood coating his tongue and leaking out the corner of his mouth as his eyes seemed to lose focus.

He released her hand, smearing blood across it, dropping his hand to the floor with a thunk. They turned for the door as a figure stepped in front of it. They wore a saturated black hoodie, more red splattered across their skull mask than Ryan's. This figure was tall, but not close to Ryan's height, and their bloody Bowie hunting knife dripped with blood as they raised it before them.

Fox pulled Jack back, her heart caught in her throat as every cell in her body tingled, forcing her to move. The figure grabbed Jack, yanking her away from Fox, coughing. A man. He twisted her into his grip, pressing her back against his chest and the knife against her neck.

"No," Fox gasped, reaching forward.

Jack cried out, and Fox stopped, wincing in pain as if she'd felt the knife dig into her own flesh. The figure nodded in Fox's direction once, then twice, slowly. He wanted her to back up.

"Don't hurt her." Fox took a step back, raising her hands as he seemed to lower the blade slightly. Jack leaned forward. The figure nodded again, and she took another step back, closer to Scott. The figure lowered the knife a little more.

She stared at Jack, trying to get her to focus. "It's going to be okay."

Where are Costa and Kerry? What happened downstairs?

In her eyes, she told Jack they were going to keep going. Just keep going until they found their moment to run.

Fox took another step back, knocking her foot against Scott's leg. Shaking, she checked behind her. Pressing her hand against the wall for support, she cleared his body, stopping between Scott and Ryan. As she turned back, the figure lowered the knife completely and pulled a gloved hand up, holding something gray in it—a cloth?

He covered Jack's mouth with it, shoving it up against her nose. Jack screamed and flailed her arms and legs, dropping slightly. Fox moved to lunge forward, but the figure held the knife up again, shaking his head no as Jack twitched, slouching in his grasp.

She had to get help. She couldn't let them be the only ones left alone with this knife-wielding murderer.

As Jack's body movements slowed down, Fox braced for her to slump over. If she ran, she might surprise him, and he'd have to come after her. She couldn't let him hurt Jack. As Jack's body went limp, the figure released her, letting her slump to the floor beside Scott.

Fox turned and ran down the hallway, through the kitchen, and flung the back door open. She jumped through it onto the patio, hard rock thumping from the speaker beside the hot tub. She took a left and ran past the hot tub; the back of someone with short, blonde hair, floating face down amongst the pink bubbles. She bolted toward the corner of the house, unwilling to let the body distract her. She couldn't help them anymore, but she had to save Jack. She glanced over her shoulder before she rounded the corner of the house, the masked figure following in her peripheral vision as déjà vu filled her, chilling her.

She had to get to the neighbour's house.

As she ran, a cough echoed behind her. The same cough she heard the night before at work. He'd been watching her. Whoever was doing this had been watching her, waiting for something.

She emerged from the darkness between the two houses and pushed herself toward the right, to her old home, toward the neighbour's driveway. Surprising tension turned to pain as she was yanked in a backward motion by her hair. She stumbled back, staggering as the pressure released, and the figure stepped to the side, blocking the sight of her old house. He lifted his knife high, the clean spots on the blade glinting by the moonlight, and brought it down as she pushed herself back. Falling backward and grasping at the nothingness in front of her, her stomach flipped. The knife grazed her forearm, slashing through her flesh before she landed on her side with a thud, releasing a short cry.

The figure stepped toward her, knife in hand, and she scrambled back on her hands and butt, closer to Jack's house, to the driveway. Her hip throbbed, but she couldn't feel any pain on her arm. She had to get to the neighbour's, but he wouldn't expect her to go back inside the same house.

As the figure stepped closer, he tucked the knife into a cover and behind his back. He raised a clenched fist into the air, bending down toward her as she held her hands in front of her face for protection. As the fist came down on the side of her head, the gray world spun before her. She fell to the grass, the back of her head hitting the cold dirt beside Jack's driveway. She closed her eyes as a sharp, searing pain shot through her head, fast as lighting.

As her eyes fluttered open, the figure reached down and grabbed her, pulling her up. She tried to push against him, tried to pull back so he couldn't lift her, but she could barely breathe. The world blurred before her tear-filled eyes as she opened her mouth, gasping for air. The figure picked her up—coughing, wheezing—and dragged her.

Across the grass toward the driveway.

Across the asphalt, her back burning hotter by the inch.

He leaned her against a vehicle, cradling her against his leg as he opened the door. What door, she couldn't tell. She couldn't even tell which car as he hoisted her in the back. Her vision darkened as a slumped figure sat in the passenger's seat before her, the head with short hair tilted at an unnatural angle, unmoving.

Elisha.

The door slammed shut.

"Help," she sputtered, reaching out for her friend.

As her fingers connected with Elisha's cold arm, she grasped it. Elisha's head rolled off her body and out the side window.

Fox's heart pounded in her chest as she gasped for air, for help, in shock and in fear, but she couldn't inhale. She couldn't move. And she couldn't keep her eyes open.

26

Fox opened her eyes in darkness, turning her head toward the tiny sliver of light shining a beam on her slashed arm. It stung like her head, but as she shifted, she realized she was in a small, dark space. She peered out through the crack of the two open back doors as panic fluttered in her chest, beating its wings, demanding to be released. The back of a van —*Ryan's van?*

Both sliding doors to the warehouse sat open. She was at Haskin's. The single, long tube of fluorescent light in the middle shone down on two chairs beneath it, facing each other.

She pushed herself up, leaning against the side of the van, scanning the inside up by the front seats. Empty. She had to get out. She had to get help.

Muffled voices echoed from inside the warehouse. She couldn't make them out, but she thought she heard Jack's voice—Jack crying. Her stomach twisted, and she winced at the pain in her head as she pushed herself to her hands and knees. She slowly crawled to the front of the van and pulled herself up using the back of the driver's seat.

"Not long now," a voice called. "You'll have to make a decision. Whose life is more important?"

Whoever was behind the skull mask was distracted, but it wouldn't be for long.

Fox climbed over the middle console, into the front seat, and held her breath as she cracked the front door open.

As she did, a flood of light illuminated the van, and then the light doubled.

"What the—" a male voice muttered.

She pushed out the door and hopped to the ground, rounding it and running toward the back shop door where the large rock sat, propping it open. She didn't chance looking back. She had to get inside before they caught her. She heaved the door open just enough to slip inside, shoving the rock out of the way with her boot, and darted inside. The heavy, metal door closed behind her. She leaned against it, panting. Pressing her hand to her aching hip, she stumbled down the long, dark hallway to the front of the store.

She had to get to the front door, lock it, then use the phone to call the police.

One thing at a time, she told herself.

It's the last way they can get in. The only way left.

She staggered down the hallway, a slight limp in her stride as she burst into the front shop and down the middle aisle. She made it to the door as the figure in the skull mask—glowing neon red beneath the sign—ran across the front window on the other side of the glass. He reached it at the same time she reached for the lock and twisted it.

The Skull craned his neck back and cocked his head to the side.

She slammed her palm against the glass, right where his face was.

Beat you.

She shuffled backward, safe inside, but Jack and whoever else was out there needed help. They needed her.

Out there, past The Skull, sat Luke's white patrol car along the curb. Hope leaped from her chest one second and evaporated in another. If he was still here, protecting the store, this wouldn't be happening. And Kennedy. She'd never received her text that Kennedy had gotten home safely.

Fox ran to the front counter and grabbed the mouse, but the computer screen remained dark. She checked the cords at the back, following them beneath the counter to where they'd been cut.

Sidestepping along the edge of the counter toward the hallway, The Skull walked in front of the glass, mirroring her the whole way. *How thick is that glass? How easily could it break?* She didn't have time to consider it with Jack in danger out there. She ran down the hallway, stumbling into the office, and picking up the landline. No dial tone. She hadn't expected one, but she had to check.

Backing out of the office, she looked down the hallway where the bright red exit sign glowed. *They can't get in that way. There's no way.* As long as The Skull was out front, in view through the glass, she had a way out. She walked toward it, passing the bathroom on her right when light reflected off something wet on the floor. Dark liquid seeped out from beneath the bathroom door, glowing by the neon exit sign.

She held her breath and pushed it open, picturing Luke's body by the stalls. She squinted, expecting darkness. The warm, fluorescent lights atop each of the three mirrors illuminated the words written in blood on them, but her stare dropped to the floor.

Kennedy lay sprawled on her back on the mint tile, something like Scott's position earlier, bleeding from a singular spot on her chest. Fox pressed her hand to her mouth, swallowing back at the lump in her throat, over and over. She was going to be sick. A bullet wound? So much blood. It pooled on the floor, making it impossible to hop over if she wanted to go inside, but she didn't need to get any closer to see the words on the mirror.

They paid the toll twice.

Kennedy? Did The Skull think Kennedy did something to him? It doesn't make sense—what toll?

She bent down, and like Jack, she patted the sides of Kennedy's pockets on the off chance she'd been left with a cell phone. Saliva pooled in her mouth, and she swallowed it down, ready to be sick at any moment. As she patted, she only felt the shape of Kennedy's hips, front to back. Kennedy's eyes stared up at the ceiling, wide in terror. The sequined, cat-ear headband sat a few feet from her body by the first stall. Fox turned her head away, the vision remaining as she stood and staggered back, away from the body and out into the hallway.

The door swung closed, Fox's chest heaving, and she turned back down the hallway toward the storefront. *The Skull.* She crept toward it, needing to see The Skull was still there. That he wouldn't be waiting at the back door—her only real chance at escape.

Once she got out, what could she do? Where could she run? There weren't any businesses close enough to get help from. Maybe Luke was still there, or maybe he'd gone for help. She couldn't rely on anyone else.

If anyone had the chance to leave, she was glad, but she'd stay.

It was decided in an instant, like second nature.

She had to free Jack, and they could hide together. She knew the property so well; she could navigate it blindfolded. She had the advantage there. But if Jack was able, they could run and get to a safe place, or just outrun The Skull. That's all they had to do.

All she had to do was get Jack.

She pressed herself against the inside wall, closest to the counter before the back wall at the storefront, and peered around the corner. An engine revved, echoing through the front lot. *A car? Is someone here?* She stepped out from the hallway, walking toward the counter and scanning the front window. No Skull.

She blinked, and the room filled with light—headlights shining directly into it, but not directly in her eyes. She stepped forward, squinting as Luke's car shielded some of the front shop from the lights beyond. A crunching sound shocked her back into focus and sent her stumbling back as a louder crunching followed. Luke's white car rolled on its side toward the front window. A tinny, high-pitched *pop* sent her stumbling back as the car crashed through the front shop window, sending glass shattering, flying through the air.

Fox turned and ran down the hallway as more bangs and crashes echoed in the front shop behind her.

Get out—get out and get Jack.

She crashed into the metal bar along the back door and swung it open, lunging through it. Black arms reached out for her, and The Skull wrapped them around her, pushing a white cloth over her mouth.

She screamed, pressed between his arms and hard chest. She flailed her arms, kicking and elbowing at the man behind her, inhaling deeply against her will. Desperate for the energy to fight back, she cried out.

The glow from the open warehouse doors became a cool, soft crush of colour before her eyes as they fluttered closed.

She gasped for breath, suddenly recognizing the pungent scent of ammonia as she took one more breath.

The darkness came fast—too fast for her to think of anything other than Jack.

27

"Fox." Jack's voice came as a whisper, if she'd really heard it at all.

Through her blurry vision, Jack appeared, leaning over her, a soft smile on her face.

"Jack?" she muttered, turning over on her back as her head throbbed, blinking up as her cousin disappeared. "Jack?"

Fox moaned, squeezing her eyes shut and wiping at them with her fingers to ease the tension away. As her eyes fluttered open, her vision still blurry, someone else whispered to her.

"I'm here."

Before she could ask who it was, the familiar voice, low and gruff, registered as her dad's.

"Dad?" she whispered, pushing herself to sit.

She blinked past the checkered links of the storage cage in the warehouse to the two chairs facing each other in a pool of light. Jack sat on one, her hands tied behind the chair. The cool, fluorescent light shone off the electrical tape covering her lips, and her eyes found Fox's, wide with fear and concern.

"Your arm's bleeding," someone whispered from a dark corner behind her.

Fox turned to Scott, sitting in the shadows, his hair coated and matted in blood. She checked her arm, the long cut along the back of it still wet with blood. She pressed her fingers to it and let out a hiss. *How long was I out? What happened?*

The crash.

The car crashed through the shop window. *But how did The Skull do that and reach the back of the building in time to grab me?*

"How did we get here?" Fox asked, blinking up at Scott through the pain in her head.

His face was a welcome sight, despite the blood. He survived.

Scott turned to the other dark corner.

She followed his stare to someone standing in the shadows—a man.

The figure walked from the darkness toward her. She twisted her body to face him.

He stopped, and his face began to come into focus. His thick, dark hair and beard. Slate Cornell.

His long-sleeved denim button-up had blood on the collar, appearing to have dripped from his nose, where clotted, crusty blood rested in the recesses of his nostril. His hands were empty, but his deep stare frightened her as he loomed over her.

"What do you want with us?" Fox whispered. "It's me you're after, isn't it? I don't know what I've done, but don't hurt her." She turned to Jack, who watched on in silence.

Slate didn't speak. He only stood, staring at them, then glancing behind him at Scott and back to them.

"I'm so sorry for what happened to your daughter——" Fox used her hands to push herself up to her feet, putting distance between them as she approached the front of the cage that kept her from Jack.

Her vision blurred, her heavy head dizzy with the movement.

Slate reached out to her. "Don't get too close."

His voice was barely above a whisper, but she didn't miss the sharpness behind the warning. She inched out from within his grasp. Scott joined her side.

"He's been locked in here longer than we have." Scott rubbed at the back of his head, his fingers coated in blood as he reached out for the cage. "He made me tie her up. He—he checked to make sure it was tight enough."

"The man in the skull mask?" she asked, turning to Jack.

"Yes," he muttered beside her, hanging his head.

"Let us go!" she shouted, slamming her palm against the cage links over and over.

Jack bent at her waist, her sobs muffled by the tape as her body shook. Panic welled in Fox's chest again as her surroundings came into full focus.

No one appeared. The double doors remained closed.

She turned to Scott and Slate. "Where is he? *Who* is he?"

Slate looked past her, seemingly at Jack. "He's the man who killed my daughter."

"How did you get here?" she asked.

He shook his head. "I don't know. I was on my way home yesterday, and when I got there... It was my first time being back there since... and I just... I drank, and then I fell asleep, and I woke up here hours ago."

"Why?" Fox asked. "Why would someone do this?"

"Because it's time to pay the toll." A voice came from the other side of the room, in the shadows, and she recognized the words from the streaks painted across the mirror in poor Kennedy's blood.

Slate turned his back to them and stepped closer to the bars of the cage. "Show your face, you fucking coward!"

Something hard knocked against the floor, rolling toward the bottom of the cage. It clanged to a stop against it, between where she and Slate stood.

Fox squinted past the pain in her head at the heart-shaped stone leaning against the caged area.

"You know who it is," the deep male voice said, taking a step forward. "You all know me, in one way or another."

She recognized the voice, but she couldn't tell from where.

He took another step forward, the fluorescent light illuminating a figure in a black hoodie, wearing the skull mask she'd seen before.

She'd seen it that night with Costa near the warehouse.

She'd seen it staring at her in the middle of the road

at the party, probably right after he'd tampered with her dad's truck, causing the breakdown.

She'd seen it when the man behind it invaded her home, attacked her friends, stole her cousin, and shoved Fox in a vehicle with the decapitated Elisha.

Others wore similar masks, but none were just like his.

The Skull stepped further into the light between the chairs, just a few feet from Jack.

With both gloved hands, he reached behind his head and pulled the mask off. "It's time to pay the toll, and you're gonna pay twice."

28

The man ran his hand back and forth over his short, brown hair, clutching the mask in his other gloved hand. Dirt streaked across the corner of his mouth, as if he'd been eating it, the mental image both disturbing and fitting all at once. He looked to be in his mid-fifties, and as Fox squinted at him, she still couldn't recognize him.

What was she missing?

"You're probably wondering why you're here. I'll tell you the same thing I told the others." He turned to Jack and looked her up and down, walking around her, seeming to inspect the ropes tied around her wrists. "For all intents and purposes, *you* did nothing wrong."

As he walked back to the space between the chairs, his focus still on Jack, the light shone on his skin—on the dirt that wasn't dirt. It was remnants of black-and-orange face paint.

"Jacob?" Fox sputtered. "You... you pretended to be Elisha's boyfriend? You killed her!"

She couldn't bring herself to say how because the method was so grizzly, she'd scare Jack even worse if she shared it.

Jack turned to Fox, her eyes wide in terror.

"I didn't pretend to be her boyfriend." He mocked, pulling the cover off one of the vehicles behind him, revealing Luke, mouth taped and hands tied behind his back. "In fact, for Elisha, that would have been impossible. She thought I was married, which *really* helped explain why I could never have her over and why we couldn't get too emotionally invested."

"Luke!" Fox shouted to him.

He released a deep, muffled cry.

Jacob shook his head and pulled a gun from behind his back, walking toward Luke and aiming it at him. "This one got too close last night, and then interrupted my painting session in the bathroom."

"Leave him—" Fox screamed.

A gunshot rang through the air as he shot Luke point-blank in the head. Luke fell backward onto the vehicle cover with a soft *whoosh* and then a *thud*.

Fox screamed and pressed her hands to her mouth, shaking her head. *This isn't happening—can't be happening. What the hell is happening?*

"He inserted himself in our lives," Slate said, staring at him. "You wore a bracelet like the rest of us. Were you even admitted, or was that part of the plan?"

The man smiled, unmoving. "I spent some time there myself a year ago for circumstances not unlike your own. Been there, kept the bracelet."

The way he taunted them, seemingly living in a place between amusement at their pain and annoyance at their existence, confused her. How could he speak like that after he just shot Luke?

Luke was dead, and Kennedy, too. He'd used her blood to write on the mirror.

And Elisha. He'd used Elisha. She'd trusted him, and he'd disposed of her.

Her stomach clenched at each realization hitting her over and over.

"Are you really a professor? Or did you just pretend to be... to get closer to her?" Fox shouted indignantly. *He didn't care about them, so why did he have to kill them?* "Why? What did she do? You just said Jack did nothing! Let her go!"

"Not to get closer to her." He shook his head. "To get closer to *you*. How did you think I knew about your Halloween tradition?" He turned to Slate. "And *you*. You, I had to see for myself, without the mask. Daughterless father to daughterless father. How does it feel?"

Slate smacked the cage with his palms, rattling it, releasing a guttural scream.

Daughterless father. One year ago, Victoria Castle died in a car accident on Halloween, but her father—his name wasn't Jacob.

"We had to watch, didn't we?" The man took a step toward the cage, and then another. "We were right there, and we could have looked away, but we watched our daughters' lives slip away. You watched your poor Piper, and there was nothing you could do about it." The man clenched his gloved hands into fists. "Nothing could be worse, could it? That's what I wanted to know when I saw you the other day in the hospital. I wanted to know if it tortured you like it does me. I had to make sure you left that place, and I had to make sure you weren't numb, like you were doing with the alcohol before you checked yourself in. I had to sober you up for this. You know, I never touched the bottle after Victoria." His voice shook for the first time. "*Never.* I'm not weak like you. I had to feel it, and now, so do you. Both of you."

"Victoria? Castle? You're her father?" Fox whispered. Slate turned to her, then back to the man, his face twisted in confusion. "Victoria died in a car accident last year—"

"Don't *ever* say her name!" the man shouted, but the man wasn't Jacob, like he'd told Elisha and possibly even the college. It was John, like the obituary said. "I wanted this to be different—for all of you. I wanted to make this as close to what I experienced—as painful as possible. But the only way to do that was time. Time and your own memories of watching the one you love most murdered in front of you can torture you more than I ever possibly could."

That's why he has Jack. Her fingers trembled at her sides, her heart pounding like the panic fluttering in her chest, desperate to be released.

He took another step closer to Slate, just a few feet away. "I tried, last month, to carry out the plan when I killed Piper in front of you, but there was a witness. The police got there too soon. That's when I knew I couldn't take the chance again—not for my Victoria."

"You fucking bastard!" Slate screamed, banging on the cage. "She was innocent! She did nothing wrong!"

"Neither did my Victoria." The man shook his head and turned to Jack. "You would have been next. And then the mayor's whore. And then the three of you would have suffered for a year, maybe more. And I'd have a front-row seat. Shortly after I discovered the role you all played, I inserted myself into your lives. I found out who you loved most. I learned your routines—"

Jack was going to die because of Fox. Adrenaline shook through her veins as she gripped the metal cage separating her from her cousin.

"Let her go," Fox wailed.

John only smiled and turned to Jack.

That other empty chair—*it has to be for me.* She was sure John had made all his other victims watch each other before he'd killed them. He was going to let her out of the cage, and that would be her chance.

"Fox loves you more than anyone." John turned back to Slate. "And you loved your daughter more than anything. And the mayor loved his mistress almost as much as he loved himself... He was more difficult. You work with what you have, though, and I've gathered *so much* to work with."

"What did we do to you?" Fox screamed. "Our role in what?"

"He's sick! He's a maniac!" Slate shouted at her. "There's no reason—"

"There's a reason." The man reached behind him and pulled a handgun from his back pocket. "There are three. Last Halloween Eve, I'd gotten home from work and my daughter was waiting for me. She asked if I'd do her a favour. We shared a car, and she knew I had a work event at the college the next night, but she said she'd got a last-minute gig with her new modelling agency. She asked if I'd drive her to the studio before I left, then pick her up on my way home. We made a plan for Halloween night—a last-minute plan, thanks to you."

The Halloween night she'd gotten in her accident.

He nodded to Fox. "But I'm sure you've figured it out for yourself by now, working at the same studio."

"What studio?" Slate asked.

"I changed my shift," she whispered, turning to Slate and then Scott. "For the Halloween event here. We were all required to work, so I had to call and let the studio know I couldn't do the shoot that night." She turned to John. "I found out last minute—"

"So did my Victoria. That night, the storm was so bad my event got canceled, but Victoria said she *needed* to go to the shoot, and she could lose out on that opportunity and future ones if she didn't go. You put her in a bad place, Fox. I didn't want us to go, and if I had known what she was really doing, I'd have never let her go back there again, and I'd have..." He licked his lips, the cool light reflecting off the tears welling in his eyes. "Before the snow melted, I found the owners of the studio, and I made those brothers watch each other die. I didn't know what she was doing... I didn't know, and that night, she insisted it was important to her. I'd have done anything she needed from me—anything she'd asked. So we went, and it was all because of you." He raised his gun, aiming it at Fox, then lifted it slightly, pretending to shoot her before returning it to his side.

"The roads in this town are terrible on a good day, but they were so slick that night, I was slipping around. The mayor has a budget in this town for the roads, and after some research, I discovered he'd been pocketing it for himself, his mansion, his lifestyle, and even his mistress from time to time, though not nearly the amount she'd spent on him. The potholes and sunken spots in the road were so bad that night... We were halfway there when Victoria realized how dangerous it was. She said we should just go home, but I knew how much the shoot meant to her, and what the fallout could be if she didn't show. I carried on."

He aimed the gun at Slate. "Do you remember where you were on Halloween night last year?"

Slate didn't speak. He stared indignantly at him, as if daring him to shoot him right then and there.

John took a step toward him, pressing the gun against the cage. "I do. Maybe drinking isn't a new thing for you. Maybe you were drinking that night. I'll never know because you got away with it."

"Away with what?" Fox whispered.

"We were rounding the bend on Black Creek Road, and an SUV was stopped in front of us, in the middle of the dark road, no blinkers on—nothing. I braked—too hard. I swerved..." He lowered his head, and as it rose again, his eyes squinted shut. He shook away whatever thought or memory he'd conjured and opened his eyes, focusing on Slate staring down the barrel of his gun.

"This drunk sent us into the ditch, just to avoid colliding with him."

"I wasn't drinking! I didn't drink when I had Piper! You! You did this—"

John shook his head, shouting above Slate, "Then why'd you stop? Why would you stop in the middle of the goddamned road in a rainstorm? No hazard lights! No warning! You gave us no warning, and now, we'll save you for last!"

His voice echoed through the warehouse.

Fox shook her head, stepping away from the cage. "It was an accident! It was all just an accident! No one wanted to hurt your daughter!"

"But you did." His calm tone returned. He lifted the gun slightly, pretending to shoot Slate. "And now, you'll pay your final toll."

Jack's muffled cries caught John's attention, and he glanced over his shoulder. "But first..."

"There's nothing you can do to me!" Slate shouted. "Nothing!"

"You'll watch them die, just like your daughter," John said, walking toward Jack. "And then you'll pay your debt. It's not about hurting you anymore. It's about making things right—it's all we've got left. I'm going to make it right, Vic."

Scott moaned in the corner and staggered to the side, wincing as he leaned against the wall. He covered his face with his bloody hands and rocked back and forth.

"What about him?" Fox pointed to Scott. "What did he do?"

"Let's just say things didn't go according to plan

tonight. Your friends got in my way." He looked at Scott with a stoic expression and lowered his voice. "There can't be *any survivors*."

"You killed them all, didn't you?" Fox shouted. "Elisha and... Oh, C-Costa. Kerry and Ryan. Kennedy." Chills crept beneath her skin until her whole body shook as she remembered the thud Luke's body made when he fell after John shot him.

"Oh, God," Scott groaned, bending at the waist as he rocked himself back and forth.

John watched on, his harsh gaze remaining on Scott. "No more witnesses. It ends tonight. Time to wake up. Time for Fox to watch the one she loves most bleed out before her. I warn you, you'll never experience anything worse."

A harsh wheeze escaped his lips, and he laughed until he coughed, shaking his head and pulling something from his pocket.

He was going to release her—it was all starting, and she couldn't stop it.

"No," Fox screamed, stepping back from the cage.

"You're afraid. You should be. Watching the life bleed out of the one you love most..." John turned to Slate. "Well, you can tell her how it feels."

Slate banged the side of his fist against the cage once more, turning back to them, panting. "I won't—I won't let him do this."

"You're going to tie her up now," John said, producing a key between the pinched fingers of his glove.

Scott pushed himself off the wall, dropping his hands

from his face. "I'm sorry, Fox. I tied her up, and now—Oh, God, I'm so sorry."

"Please, don't," Fox whispered, grabbing his arm. "He won't let you live, no matter what he's told you."

Scott pressed his lips together, turning away from her. Slate paced along the back wall of the cage like a trapped animal, desperate for escape. Everything and everyone crumbled around her except John. Everything was going according to his plan. She had to stall him.

John had visited Slate to ensure he left the facility in time for his part. He'd inserted himself into Fox's life through Elisha, but how had he known Jack would be there for Halloween that night, even if he'd somehow managed to get her to tell him it was tradition?

"How," she muttered, unsure where to go from there, but she had to make it up on the fly. She needed more time. Her eyes searched the room for a weapon as she spoke. "How did you know Jack would be here?"

"You're always together on Halloween," John said, walking toward the cage with his key. "I played a hunch that she'd be back, but if not, I'd have brought her back. She just made it easy for me. You're all so predictable with your traditions and vices."

He turned to Slate. "You couldn't save your daughter. You won't be able to save them."

For the first time, Slate ignored him instead of taking the bait, continuing to pace in the shadows.

"Scott"—Fox turned to him, leaning close as John approached—"you need to get ready to fight. We have to save her. We need to get out of here."

John slipped his key into the lock.

"You can't do this!" Fox shouted. "Victoria wouldn't want you to kill people, would she?"

"I told you not to say her name." John's hand stopped before twisting it unlocked. "You don't tell me what she'd want. What she'd want is to be alive! What we need is to do the only thing left to do—I have to do the only thing I can now for us. My only regret is that your suffering won't be as prolonged as ours."

Scott stumbled forward, standing shoulder to shoulder with Fox. "I'm ready."

Fox wasn't sure if he was addressing her or John.

The metal keys jingled as he twisted the lock open and pointed the gun at Fox. "You're going to tie her up, just like Jack. You're going to want to do *exactly what I tell you*."

John nodded to Slate. "Move back, or I shoot this one in the head right now."

Slate took a step back.

"Further," John said, nodding like he had in the front hallway of Jack's house while he held Jack against him.

Slate took one more step back, giving Fox a look with wide eyes. He was going to act while they still had a chance. She believed him when he said he wouldn't let them die—that John could take no more from him. Slate would try to save them, even if it meant his own death. A man with nothing left to lose was dangerous, and she had to anticipate the actions of two of them.

She nudged Scott's arm subtly as John opened the cage door. He kept the gun aimed at Fox and stepped back, allowing them room. "Let's go!"

Fox took a step forward, as close to the door as Slate

was. She made eye contact with him, her eyes pleading for a hint about his plan, for something to act on, for hope that they could work together to save each other as Scott wrung his hands beside her.

Slate clenched his jaw, his nostrils flaring. He turned to John with a darkness in his eyes, charging at him.

John aimed his gun at Slate. A bang exploded beside her, echoing through the warehouse.

29

Screaming. They were all screaming, or was it just Fox? She couldn't tell until she stopped and opened her eyes, letting her hands fall from her ears. Blood spurted from the wound in Slate's leg as he writhed in pain on the cement floor a foot away.

John's skull mask was back on, and he turned the gun from Slate to Fox. "Get out here, now!"

They'd lost Slate as an asset—their best hope at overpowering John—and they'd done nothing when John shot him. She'd been paralyzed with fear, the gunshot still ringing in her ears, her jaw clenched as pain rang inside her head.

As soon as they left the cage, they'd be more vulnerable and exposed than when they were inside it—and closer to death. She knew it in her bones, yet as she took her first step forward, she focused on Jack. Black mascara stained the skin around her eyes as she blinked at Fox, shaking her head no. Every step she took without a plan was a step closer to their deaths, and John had made it clear—Jack would go first. He wanted Fox to watch it happen. He was intent on it. Maybe so intent, he wouldn't stand for another order of operations.

What did they need? To get out alive. There were two ways out—through the sliding doors along the wall at Jack's back, or the side door to the left of the cage in the same direction. If she could lure him as far away from the door as possible, even if he thought he was cornering her, the others could leave. She could bring him there, to the corner by the kayaks, and Scott would have time to untie Jack, but could Slate make a run for it without the help of the others? Would they leave him behind? Could she?

If it meant saving Jack's life, she could. She needed to create a distraction. She needed to share something from the most secretive parts of her life—the naked, vulnerable parts no one was supposed to find out about.

Fox stepped out of the cage with Scott following behind her.

"You—you," Slate sputtered on the floor, his hands pressing against his leg as he winced at them, pain filling his eyes.

John shook his head and sighed. "What about me? You're pathetic, you know that? And after your recent psychiatric stay, and all the trauma inflicted upon you, no one will question that you could have snapped and did all this."

"Fuck you!" Slate spat.

"Fuck *them*." He laughed. "People with mental health issues are far more likely to be harmed than to harm others, but *their* stigma is *my* get-out-of-jail-free card."

Anger welled in her chest, thrumming just beneath her skin. She took deep breaths, tuning them out, focusing on the objective to not only get John's attention, but ensure it stayed on her.

She turned over her shoulder to Slate, waiting until he made eye contact with her as a puddle of blood grew beneath his leg on the concrete.

She opened her eyes wide and mouthed "Get ready to go."

He rocked back and forth in pain, his gaze moving to the ceiling, and she hoped he understood—and that he was ready to at least try.

As she stepped out, John nodded to the empty chair and took a step back toward the side door. "Tie her up," he said, coughing. "And do it right this time. You know I'll be checking."

Fox took another step toward one of the chairs and turned to John, making eye contact with him when she stopped. "I don't think your daughter would—"

He took a step forward, aiming his gun at her. "I told you not to talk about her—"

Good. The sore spot. I'll stick myself right in it.

She remained still, speaking calmly. "I don't think she'd want you to treat her friend like this."

"Her *what?*"

"I was friends with your daughter. We started out as co-workers, just models who could relate to the issues in the industry, who were afforded the opportunity to make larger sums of money in short periods of time, and then we became friends."

"She never said anything about you. Keep moving."

He turned to Scott. "Hey, get her tied up!"

"I never spoke about my friends at work to anyone in my life except my cousin." She nodded to Jack and raised her brows. "They made us sign NDAs and contracts about anonymity, but I told Jack about Victoria."

John turned to Jack, keeping the gun aimed at Fox. She used the moment to take a quick step to the side, toward the kayak rack in the back corner.

Jack nodded, her gaze drifting to her cousin until Fox shook her head and took another step further. Jack focused back on John. She moaned, seeming desperate to tell him something behind her taped lips.

"Okay, so you were friends." John turned back to Fox. "That's why she took your shift so eagerly for you? Because she wanted to help out a friend? Is that what friends do? They dump their responsibilities on each other? No, I'm not buying it. I would have known. You didn't even go to her funeral."

Fox sighed, calming her nerves as she took another step away, taking control of the conversation. "That's because she didn't have one. Was that a trick question, Jacob. I'm sorry, Mr. Castle? Or should I call you John? She never called you that, but she told me your name when I told her about how I lost my dad."

He cocked his head to the side, that same eerie move he'd done to her before she'd known who was beneath the mask. She couldn't tell what was going on behind there, but she knew she had his attention.

He turned toward Jack and Scott, who'd remained closer to John. "Did she know my daughter?"

Good, he was questioning. She took another step backward, toward the corner as Jack nodded. Maybe she could use one of the kayak paddles to defend herself once she got there. What was something else she could say about Victoria? Something she'd seen in the article and obituary. She couldn't remember anything except...

"I don't have any tattoos," Fox said, taking a step toward the opposite side of the room, hoping he'd read into it and assume she was trying to put as much space between them as possible. "I was advised they're bad for the business of modelling, not to mention the fact that it doesn't help when you want to be kept anonymous, but your daughter had them, and she was proud of them. I admired her for that. That bird on her back was beautiful."

"Shut the fuck up, and get back over here," John shouted, turning the gun on Jack to his left. Fox froze. He nodded to Scott. "Get the rope, or she dies now."

She approached the empty chair slowly, each pace draining the remaining hope she'd had for her plan. Scott grabbed the rope beside Jack, doing as he was told, and looked up at Fox. Her chest heaved with the weight that seemed insurmountable as she struggled to breathe, shaking her head at him.

She had to make John come closer. She had to give him a reason. She could still do it.

"Nice and tight," John said, although he didn't take his eyes off Fox. "Take your seat."

As soon as that rope was around her wrists, it would be over. If he wanted her to sit, he'd have to come and make her. He'd have to drag her to the chair, and that would give them time. With her back to Jack, he wouldn't kill her. Fox dropped to her knees and pushed herself over, her side against the cement, facing the wall opposite the double sliding doors.

"I'd prefer it if you watched," John said. "But as long as you can hear her scream to death, be my guest."

"No!" Fox struggled to stand again, desperately hoping Scott would do something—say something. "Don't do it!"

She turned around on her feet as The Skull pulled his knife from behind his back, holding it in his left hand with his gun against Jack's head. Scott stood with the rope, staring at Jack, frozen.

"Wait!" Fox shouted. "We can—we'll do this your way."

Was she buying time, hoping something else would come to her—or prolonging the time she had left with her cousin, her best friend in the world? She wasn't sure, but as she shuffled slowly toward the empty chair, it felt like the only thing she had left to do.

"Grab the rope!" he shouted at Scott as Fox approached Jack. "Don't go near her!"

Scott approached the side of the empty chair as Fox reached the back of it, stepping toward the other side between the cage and the chair. Their eyes met, and Scott's apologetic stare broke her. He was going to do as he was told. She drew a staggered breath, tears spilling down from her blurry eyes over her hot cheeks. She turned her head to John, and then to Slate, still on the floor of the cage.

Slate looked up at her from his seated position, pressing both bloody hands against his leg wound. She gave a small shake of her head, then released a cry of defeat, gasping as she drew in a shaky breath and turned to finally face Jack.

Her eyes, filled with fear, were fixed on the masked man's knife pointed at Fox, glinting in the bright fluorescent light from above. One singular light in the darkness.

Her father's voice came to her again, like it had in the cage, only this time it was a memory.

"I'm so sorry, Jack." She took a shaky breath and turned to Slate, looking down at where he sat before her on the opposite side of the cage. "I'm so sorry."

She took a step away from the chair, closer to the cage, and another.

"Hey," The Skull called as she knelt down on the other side of the cage, opposite Slate. "Get in your seat, or I'll take my time with her."

"Can you run?" she whispered to Slate.

He nodded with a clenched jaw as she picked up the heart-shaped rock and hid it in her fist, turning toward The Skull.

Fox took a step back toward the chair, looking at Jack. "It's going to be okay. Remember, it's always coldest before the dawn." She turned to the masked man, standing still by the cage, pushing the rock in her fist toward her fingers. "It's what my dad used to tell me. I lost him when I was younger. I've always envied the relationships my friends have had with their fathers, like you and Victoria."

"That's it. That's enough!" The Skull pushed his knife into Jack's neck, and she released a muffled gasp as a single line of blood trickled toward her collar bone.

Fox winced but stopped in the middle of the light between the chairs, with John and Jack on one side, and Scott on the other.

"We used to go camping"—she turned to Jack and choked out a laugh, smiling, even as blood trickled to the collar of her pink T-shirt—"and when he'd say that, I knew he was trying to give us comfort in the only way he knew how. That's what good dads do, right? They give us strength and support when we need it most. Jack? It's almost dawn."

She looked up at the flickering fluorescent light and tossed the rock up into the air. The bulb popped, followed by the tinkling glass as the warehouse went dark, and everything happened all at once.

Jack released a muffled cry.

A banging echoed from the cage, followed by a deep, male groan. Slate was moving, making his way out.

Footsteps slapped against the cement, coming toward her, then passing her. A deep groan followed before a thud as her eyes adjusted to the lack of light. Scott wrestled with The Skull on the cement behind Jack. Fox raced to her, bending behind her and scratching at the rope for grip to untie the knots. She tore at them, and Jack shook the last of it off. Scott hadn't tied her properly. Hope filled her lungs.

A grunt behind them made her turn as a dark figure moved toward them. A gunshot rang out through the warehouse. Fox pulled Jack away from the chair, knocking it over as The Skull stepped toward them, the gun aimed at them. Slate wrapped his arms around him from behind and jumped on him, pulling him to the ground, hollering in pain. Or was that John?

"Are you okay?" Fox whispered.

"Mhm," Jack whimpered, pressing her fingers against her neck with one hand as she dropped the tape and rubbed at her lips with the other. The sound of her voice flooded Fox with every ounce of energy she needed. "Come on."

They staggered toward the side door, past the glob of black wrestling on the floor.

"Scott," Jack whispered, grabbing his hand. "Let's go."

"No!" Slate's voice echoed as the muffled sound of punches came from their right, or was it the gun meeting flesh and bone?

"Wait," Scott hissed, pressing his hand against his shoulder where a dark spot grew.

In his other hand, he held the rope and passed it to Jack, seemingly in a stupor, before lunging through the darkness. He grabbed the back of Jack's knocked over chair, groaning in pain as he hobbled toward the men on the ground. The Skull looked over his shoulder, sitting atop an unmoving Slate. Scott swung the chair through the air, smashing it across The Skull's face. The Skull fell back, toppling off of Slate. Scott brought it back up in the air again, bringing it down on the masked man's chest over and over, getting closer and closer.

"Scott," Jack hissed as they neared the side door. "We have to go."

Scott looked up and down at The Skull, bringing the chair up once more. The Skull's arm shot through the air, knife in hand, and shoved it into Scott's stomach. He dropped the chair and stumbled back, holding his stomach. He looked up at Jack with the same apologetic expression he'd given Fox. John was killing them—all of them—and help wasn't close enough.

Jack pulled her in the direction of the door, less than twenty feet away.

Leave their friend—abandon them both to save themselves?

Fox couldn't, despite Jack tugging at her hand, pleading with her.

Slate gasped and wheezed in the darkness as The Skull coughed, struggling to sit, to rise to his feet. He kept getting back up, overcoming everything to finish his mission. He'd stop at nothing to get his revenge for Victoria.

They needed keys. They had to get away. Jack was right.

"Go." Slate groaned as the masked man pushed himself to his feet.

Jack led them to the door. Fox stumbled after her, her foot knocking something on the way.

The Skull stalked toward them through the darkness, his bloody knife in his gloved hand.

Fox let go of Jack's hand, bent down, and picked up the gun.

She aimed it at his chest and took a step toward him with Jack behind her. "Get a car and get help."

"I'm not leaving you," Jack cried.

The Skull's boots pounded against the cement, charging at her. Fox aimed at his chest. She squeezed the trigger, her body forced back by the power, knocking into Jack. She steadied her from behind.

The Skull took another slow, uneasy step, stumbling forward bit by bit despite the stagger in his once sure stride.

Fox and Jack backed up against the door, Fox's gun aimed at the masked man's head this time, but his movements were jerky.

"You don't have..." The masked man coughed. "The courage... to do what... what needs to be done. You can't look fear... in the face... when you don't know what to do with it."

"Hey," Scott called from behind him. The Skull turned around. Scott rolled up his sleeves, leaving bloody streaks along his forearms, and nodded to him. "I finally know what to do with it."

He staggered toward him, grabbing The Skull's fist with the knife. He wrapped his other arm around The Skull's back and twisted the knife, driving it into the middle of The Skull's chest between their bodies. As the masked man sank to his knees on the floor, sputtering words Fox couldn't understand, Scott went with him.

"It's... not done yet." The Skull wheezed.

"I have to finish it," Scott cried, turning to them. "I will—I *will* finish it."

He pushed the knife further into the masked man's chest. John released a guttural groan.

Scott staggered back, his body convulsing. Blood from his stomach splattered on the floor. Fox rested her hands on Scott's back. He pressed his hands against his stomach wound and slumped to the floor. She eased him down and walked around him, stopping in front of The Skull, within his reach.

Fox had faced her fears before, and she'd do it again. She grabbed the top of the plastic mask and ripped it off, revealing the fullness of John Castle's dazed stare.

"You," John sputtered, his hands dropping from the knife in his chest, pressing against his bent knee, determined to stand. "Will pay."

She took a step back. Adrenaline buzzed through her body as she stared at the man who'd killed so many, and threatened to take the life of the one she loved most.

"I'll finish it." She tossed his mask to the side.

As she turned back, he pushed himself up.

Fox pressed the end of the barrel of his gun to the flesh of his forehead. His eyes opened wide as he reached for her, exposing the knife in his chest.

She grabbed the handle of the knife and squeezed the trigger.

The force of the shot pushed her back, the knife slipping loose. Blood dripped from it, and from John, and from all of them. The blood-splattered mess of brain and flesh covered them, surrounded them as he fell. Fox's hands shook with the gun and knife as she dropped them to her sides. Her whole body trembled as time stood still and her ears rang.

"Fox," Jack cried, reaching out one hand, still pressing her other bloody hand to her neck. "It's over. We have to get help for them. *Please.* Come on."

Jack pulled her arm, leading her to the door as the hazy mess of black and red swam before her blurry eyes.

It was finally time to go.

30

The irony that the horrific events which took place in that warehouse had felt more within her realm of control than anything that happened afterwards wasn't lost on Fox. Her name, face, and naked body had been spread across the news, various media outlets, and social media around the world with a different focus on the story, depending on the source. She'd been the brave survivor to some, the culprit who'd pulled all the innocent people in her life into the tragedy for others, and even a sexy vixen who'd worked her way into what she had coming. She'd been hailed a hero by a few, even going so far as to say they were fans of hers. But most made it clear that Fox needed to own some of the responsibility. She could never be their perfect victim, but she didn't care what they thought. She quickly learned there was no hope of controlling a narrative to the public—even her own.

What kept her feeling so out of control were the things she obsessed about—memories of that Halloween night. They left her feeling most helpless because the only people she cared about were traumatized, grieving, devastated, or dead.

The few times she'd left their hotel room that past week, everyone stared at her and Jack, who hadn't left her side once until she exited the hospital elevator. Jack had parted with Fox to visit Scott on the third floor after the final, successful surgery on his stomach. Fox had another visitor to see.

As she approached the nurse's station, she caught the police officer standing outside one of the rooms on the third floor of the Auburn Hills hospital, staring at her. She stopped in front of a nurse standing by a computer.

"Hi, I'm Fox Dallener, here to visit Slate Cornell." She turned to the officer. "He asked for me."

The officer nodded as the nurse rounded the counter and led her through the open door. Slate lay in the only bed in the middle of the room. His casted leg hung from a contraption above, and some extra cloth, possibly bandages, bulked out his chest area beneath his gown. His head was turned toward the window, staring at the rainy day beyond.

The nurse stopped at the foot of the bed. "Mr. Cornell, the visitor you requested is here to see you."

He turned to Fox, his eyes brightening in recognition.

What they'd been through together felt like a bonding experience of survival. She'd guessed he wanted to see her to remain connected, or to debrief about what had happened like she and Jack had with Scott so many times in their hotel room. She wondered if Slate would smile when he saw the person who worked with him to save them all, but he turned toward the window again.

"Thank you," she muttered to the nurse.

As the nurse nodded and shuffled out, he spoke. "Thanks for coming. Could you stay for a few minutes?"

"Sure." Fox took a seat on his left, his bed between her and the window. "How are you feeling?"

He didn't respond, so she set her purse on her lap and waited.

Rain pattered against the window they both stared at. A soothing, calming sound of gentle tapping filled what had begun to approach an awkward silence. Slate grabbed his cup from the tray in front of him and took a sip of water. Fox wondered if he'd eaten much—if anyone had brought him food, or a coffee, or his things from home. But he didn't have anyone—not anymore. His wife had died three years before of cancer. His daughter, Piper, had been murdered in front of him. He seemed to have no other family close enough to care for him, and when she'd first tried to be there for him the evening of November first, he wasn't accepting visitors.

She fiddled with the gold medallion on her necklace that matched Jack's. "Is there... anything I can bring you? Anything you need?"

He licked his lips and sighed, still staring out the window away from her. "I was on the road that night because I needed supplies for an art project I was working on. I'd run out of a few things, so I went to the store while Piper finished handing out some Halloween candies to the trick-or-treaters for me. It *was* raining that night, and the roads *were* bad."

He stopped, and she waited as he smoothed the bed sheet by his side with his flat palm.

"My wife and I, we loved the wildlife right here in our backyard. She loved rabbits, chipmunks, and foxes, too." He pressed his lips into what could pass as a smile, tilting his head a little toward her in recognition of her name. "But deer were her favourite. I got a tattoo of one on my back and surprised her with it on our wedding night. They were on the wallpaper of Piper's baby room—still are. They'd visit the forest in our backyard, and it was magical, and so were my wife and Piper."

He cleared his throat and winced. "That night, as I was driving, I saw a deer in the middle of the road ahead. It'd been so hard since my wife died, and that eerie Halloween night, on that desolate road—" His chest heaved. "That deer felt like a sign. I stopped well before it. I didn't notice any cars approaching, and I don't remember the crash. I must have carried on before then. That deer stood in the middle of the road in the storm and looked at me—really looked at me—before walking off into the forest."

Slate stared out the window at the gray day, although she had a feeling he wasn't focused on the rain —but instead on the memory of that deer. *Did he bring me here to try to convince me he hadn't been drunk while driving that night? Did he feel like he needed to explain himself?*

"I didn't believe what he said. If that's why you're telling me, if you want me to know the truth, I believe you."

She avoided saying his name, although she'd have

had several from which to choose. John Jacob Castle, his given name they'd learned during the investigation. The Skull Masked Murderer was a name the media had used, but since that night, they'd changed it to The Skull Serial Killer. She'd referred to him as The Skull in her own mind, because in the darkness, when he'd hunted her down, that's all he became. A skull—a monster—dehumanized and seemingly supernatural. The skull mask had given him the disguise and cover he'd needed to feel powerful, untouchable, and she knew a little something about that feeling when she'd worn hers to model. She guessed their daughters had, too.

That skull mask was the way he'd chosen to both present himself to the world and hide himself at the same time, and the detectives still hadn't been able to deduce why he'd chosen it specifically.

Slate turned to her, and she refocused when he gave her his attention. His gaunt face and long beard, thick and dark with hints of gray, suggested he'd stopped trying to take care of himself. She gripped the tops of her thighs, forcing herself to lean in instead of away at the sight of the broken man in front of her. Her chest ached, and she clenched her stomach at the thought of his wife and daughter seeing him that way.

"Since I lost Piper... I've been drinking. I'm an alcoholic now, but before, after I saw that deer, it was as if I came to life again. I felt my wife's presence with me. I felt her encouragement to appreciate the beauty in this world, and I became easier to live with for Piper. We became close again." He licked his lips and reached for the water cup, keeping his eyes on her. "Did you know my daughter?"

That deer had been the sign he'd needed to be more present for his daughter until she'd been ripped from him for that very same reason, according to John Castle's logic. Fox tried to focus on the year the hope that the deer had restored in him had given them together, but she couldn't hold onto the sight of that silver lining as her eyes met the pain in his.

"We did projects together before, we must have, but no. I didn't know your daughter. I didn't know Victoria, either. I made all that up. I'm sorry. I was just trying to distract him."

He took a sip and set the cup back on the tray. His hand shook. "Did you... When you worked at the studio... Did they ever... Did they hurt..." He pressed his lips together and turned his concern-filled gaze back to the window again, clenching his bed sheet in his fist.

"Did they ever hurt us?" she asked. He didn't move or speak. "No. They never hurt us there, or at least I never had that experience. I never felt used, or anything inappropriate like that. They treated it like a professional business, but we were in control until they closed down... and I guess we know why, now. I met one of the Kinmont brothers when I interviewed, and he made it clear we got to accept or decline the jobs, and they'd protect our identities with the masks we wore." She wondered if he'd seen any of the pictures in the news or media, then shook the thought away. "They—well, they took a lot of precautions to make sure the contracts were adhered to."

With his jaw still clenched, he released his grip on

the sheet. Maybe she could help him by giving him some peace of mind with what she knew, and what she knew was, while modeling, she was never afraid. They kept it professional, they all knew the rules, and when she'd broken them with Dylan, they'd warned him to stop. She couldn't defend the business, but she could speak to her experience.

"The photographer there made it feel like art. Maybe that sounds silly—"

"It was my job to protect her." His chest heaved, and he turned his head again to face her, his stoic expression crumbling as his chin quivered. "I couldn't save her. I was *so* close. She was right there..."

Chills rippled over her whole body with the pain and desperation in his words and tone. He pressed his lips together, his mustache covering them as he turned away once more.

Nothing could change what had happened, but she wished there was something to say to make him feel less guilt. It was John who had arbitrarily decided who should be punished for his daughter's death, and she'd found no use in trying to understand his sadistic mind.

The detectives investigating the murders were adamant that John had been planning them since shortly after his daughter's death. The different identities he'd used and his methods of killing were so well-thought-out and meticulous, the detectives were shocked that anyone had made it out of Haskin's Great Outdoor Rentals alive.

He'd made his motive clear, but as the detectives pieced together the trail of the identity leaks from Cres-

cent Moon Studios and continued a search for the bodies
of the Kinmont brothers who owned it, they'd discovered
John's first move after his daughter's death was to look
into the modelling company. As soon as he'd been
released from the Auburn Hills Centre for Mental Health
Sciences, he hunted down the brothers, stalked them,
and murdered them. The detectives explained to Fox that
he'd found a digital schedule calendar on one of their
phones—that detailed the Halloween shift switch—and
at that point he added her to his revenge list.

They hadn't found the missing witness, and they
never found any evidence to suggest that John Castle had
ever taken responsibility as the driver the night his
daughter was killed in the car crash. But Fox assumed he
had—that it had eaten him up internally until all that
was left were the mangled parts that served as a
reminder that he couldn't save her.

Images of that night, of John and Slate face to face,
resurfaced any time Fox thought about their daughters.
Slate survived so many injuries. He'd survived so much
loss. He'd survived the truth. Her own burden of guilt bit
away at her, and she worried that eventually, it would be
too much for him to bear.

"I'm so sorry about your daughter," she whispered,
clutching her necklace, her fingers finding her dad's
engineering ring. "What I said about my father was true.
I lost him when I was younger..." She took a deep breath
and folded her arms over her chest, holding herself. "I
watched him die."

His sad eyes found hers, locked with empathy in

some semblance of relatable experience they shared outside of the trauma that Halloween night.

"I miss him every day, and nothing can take the pain away, and I..." She stood and reached her hand into her jeans pocket, wrapping her fingers around the smooth, solid shape. "I know it's not the same as losing a daughter. I know there's nothing I can really say. I want you to have this."

She held the heart-shaped stone out in her palm, stepped toward the bed, and set it on his tray beside his cup of water.

His eyes opened wider as he stared from the stone back at her.

"You remember what my dad always said?"

"It's always *coldest* before the dawn?" He raised his voice, the first hint of interest and curiosity she'd heard from him.

"It meant a lot to me." She nodded to the stone. "And it's not much, but maybe that'll help you remember, too."

31

The pale, cotton-candy clouds in the distance faded into a deep, blood-orange sky. Fox and Jack lay in silence on their backs in the bed of their truck, hands beneath their heads, elbows touching.

"Where are they?" Jack whispered.

Fox sighed. "They'll be here."

The last time they saw their friends was after Elisha's funeral, when they all gathered at the park across the road from the cemetery in the middle of town. They didn't speak about what happened to them that day—only where they'd go from there.

It was in that moment that Fox told Jack she was coming with her when she left for college again after the investigation was over and they were allowed to leave. Jack had hugged her, relaxing into her arms as the rest watched on. They'd asked if Fox had a plan—if she'd thought about where she'd work, or if she'd finally decided to go to college herself.

Fox didn't know the answers, but the questions

about what she'd do and where she'd end up didn't scare her any more than the thought of leaving the only home she'd ever known, and neither scared her more than the thought of losing Jack.

The worst thing that could have happened almost did. John Castle, The Skull Serial Killer to the public and The Skull to Fox, couldn't take her cousin from her. Since that night, Fox couldn't think of anything worse than losing her, and with a taste of what it would've been like, she wouldn't waste any more time on the what ifs.

The sound of a car engine came from their right, and they slowly sat up as a white van approached, dust kicking up behind the wheels.

"Told you they'd be here," Fox said, grinning.

They climbed out of the truck bed as Scott pushed through the front door of his bungalow on his crutches and met them at the tailgate of the truck. The van parked on the street in front of Scott's garage workshop to the side of the house.

Costa climbed out of the driver's side, a big smile on his face. She'd miss that smile while she was gone. Ryan slid out of the passenger's side slowly, his body in a stiff, upright position as he shut the door and turned toward them, leaning against it.

"Aren't we supposed to be twins?" Scott called, lifting one of his crutches as he leaned against the other.

Ryan shook his head, laughing. "I'm done with those. Surprised you still need them!"

"Sorry we're late," Costa called, joining Ryan's side.

He grabbed Ryan's arm and draped it over his shoulder, helping him up the driveway awkwardly, despite their height difference.

"Had to get you a parting gift, Foxy." Ryan used his other hand to fish into his jean pocket.

He produced a small piece of folded paper and then stopped before them. He held it out to her, and for a brief moment, a memory flashed before her eyes of his bloody hand, reaching up and grabbing hers.

She shook it away and pushed off the truck, curiosity overpowering the pull to relive that moment. Her fingers brushed against his as she took the paper, but instead of his bloody hand, she recalled the crushing grip he had on hers. Was it because of the intense pain he felt, or the will—the need—to warn her? Her eyes met his, squinting into the last bits of sunlight, as if searching for the answer in them. Instead, his amused stare pulled her back to the present. She walked backward and leaned against the tailgate as she unfolded the paper.

Y.O.M.

Jack peered over her shoulder. "Yom?"

Ryan smirked and shrugged. "It's like an IOU, except... Fox knows what it means."

You owe me. After helping her find Jack, and after everything they'd gone through, he *still* expected her to be his wing woman.

Fox crumpled it up in her hand. She shoved it in her pocket, shaking her head, barely hiding her smirk.

"Next time I'm back for a visit." She smiled up at him. "Maybe."

"You got the truck all fixed?" Costa asked Scott.

Scott shook his head. "Nah, I still can't bend at the waist much yet. They took it into the shop."

Scott hadn't spoken for the rest of that night before the police and ambulances arrived at Haskin's Great Outdoor Rentals. Shortly after he'd been released from the hospital, and Jack's and Fox's parents left again, he'd invited them to stay with him instead of the hotel, until their moving day.

That first night they stayed over, Fox heard him muttering in his sleep from the other room—a nightmare. Jack went in to check on him, and the next morning, she'd told Fox they held each other until the sun came up, not sleeping, not talking, just being there for each other.

After that, he seemed a little better, especially while he was focused on his physiotherapy and getting well enough to work on his vehicles again. He joined them at Kennedy's celebration of life, and Luke's funeral after that, but he almost hadn't come to Elisha's.

He confessed to Jack and Fox that he'd woken up before he was about to be put in the van. He'd witnessed John kick Elisha's head off the driveway, across the lawn, and beneath a bush. The black smile painted on her orange face created a haunting image he couldn't shake. He'd thrown up, then John forced him in the van and knocked him out again, but his nightmares about that specific memory wouldn't stop. It haunted Fox, too, but in the waking hours.

Fox suspected he'd been beating himself up for not doing more or acting quicker. He'd tried to be brave, especially for Jack, but he wasn't a violent person. Fox hadn't thought she was either, until that night. They'd all fought for their lives, and Fox wanted to make something out of what they'd fought so hard for. It was the only thing carrying her through the days of phone calls about interviews, and comments online about her body, and the worried nature of the looks their parents gave them.

"Where's Kerry?" Scott asked.

"She's back home with my mom, waiting for us. We're all going to have dinner together. You should come, Scotty." Costa pulled Ryan closer, shaking his shoulder a bit to include him, but Ryan stared at the ground.

That night, Costa had lost a round of pool against Ryan in the basement and came up to the kitchen for drinks. On the way back down, Scott had been right behind him until Costa heard a thud. He turned around as The Skull came down the stairs toward him, his gloved hands wrapping around his throat, pushing him against the staircase wall. It was the last thing he remembered.

Ryan told the police that Costa's body came flying down the stairs, and he'd rushed to him absentmindedly, pool cue in hand, thinking he was pranking him. The Skull barrelled down the stairs at him, and Ryan got one whack in with the pool cue before John charged at him and stabbed him in the stomach with his knife.

Ryan hadn't remembered coming to, climbing the stairs, or warning them. When Fox told him he'd told them to run, Ryan seemed genuinely surprised. The doctors said his loss of memory could have been due to blood loss, lack of oxygen to his brain, or head trauma he sustained without realizing it.

When Costa woke up, seemingly alone down there, he called for help. Kerry crawled out from under the pool table. She'd been hiding there in shock the whole time. When she helped Costa upstairs, they found Ryan and called the police. They waited out front for them, and as the police began to search the house, the ambulances took them to the hospital.

Only Fox had seen the body floating in the hot tub.

Jack's ex, Cooper, had come to see her against her wishes, and he'd become collateral damage. They weren't sure what exactly happened to him between the time he arrived and when he died, but his cause of death was a slit throat. His body was taken back to his hometown. Jack was in shock for days, but as it wore off, her anger overpowered her sadness. She kept saying he never should have come, and that he never listened to her. Fox suspected the anger covered up the pain that would resurface when they got back to Jack's apartment, and she was faced with his things—their things, since they'd been living together. She wanted to be there for her through that—for Jack. She wanted to give her the same support Jack had given that night before the chaos began.

Fox stepped forward and hugged Costa.

"Have a safe drive back, okay?" Costa said. His chin sank into her shoulder and out again. He was probably nodding to Jack, the driver. "Be safe. I'm a text away."

Fox took a step back, nodding to Ryan.

"See ya." Ryan nodded as Costa helped him to the lawn beside the driveway.

Jack turned to Scott and waved him over to the other side of the truck for some privacy.

"We'll be back for Christmas break," Jack said, her voice fading in the wind. "But come see us before then, will you?"

Scott nodded and held both of her hands, staring into her eyes without saying anything.

John Castle's skull mask, Bowie hunting knife, and a handgun that was old, unregistered, and apparently untraceable were collected as evidence in the warehouse. The detectives had found a rock the size of a cantaloupe wedged between the driver's seat and floor of Slate's car. John had used it to send the car through the front shop window, and subsequently, Fox ran out the back exit where he'd waited for her.

Fox hadn't been given much more information about the investigation, but she'd noticed a pattern. John used the gun on the victims he'd had no personal vendetta against—even using his blade for them at times—but he'd stabbed his intended prey with that hunting knife and made their loved ones watch them bleed out, over and over. Haunted by that fact, she couldn't help but picture what would have happened if they hadn't stopped him. The what ifs tortured her just as much as her memories.

"Hey, those pictures of you going around," Ryan said, bringing Fox's attention back to him.

She raised her brows, wondering which ones he was referring to, and why it had taken him so long to mention them. Nothing seemed off limits to Ryan—no joke too dark, no situation too serious.

"What about them?" Fox pursed her lips, waiting for his latest take, funny joke, or maybe even a disparaging comment about her body.

Whatever he said, she could take it. After Halloween night, she felt like she could take on anything.

He squinted with a halfhearted smile. "You know you've got nothing to be ashamed about, right?"

She brought her hand to her forehead, shielding the sun from her eyes as she tried to determine if that was supposed to be a cheeky compliment or a show of support. With Ryan—without his expected cheap jokes or remarks—both were a welcome change. And that halfhearted smile seemed to hold a little more meaning than she'd thought at first glance.

Costa cleared his throat. "I think he means to say we aren't looking at them, and no decent person should. You wanted to be anonymous—"

"I'm not." She shook her head and sighed, leaning her arm against the side of the truck bed, recalling the conversation she had with Jack in her room that night. "I'm not ashamed or embarrassed, and I'm not anonymous. I always knew there was a chance this could happen. I wanted to do it, and even though I don't anymore, even though they try to use them against me, or judge my worth, or to discredit what happened to me somehow because I'm apparently not the 'perfect, innocent victim.' I don't care anymore. After what we went through, you know?"

She lowered her hand, the cranberry haze of dusk easing the pain from her eyes as she opened them wider.

Costa nodded. "That shit doesn't matter much."

He knew exactly what she meant—he'd known ever since his mother's diagnosis.

"Yeah, who cares?" Ryan asked. "Fuck 'em."

She pressed her lips together, suppressing a giggle as she brushed her hair out of her face.

"I appreciate the support." She turned her attention back to Jack and Scott.

Scott brought his hand to the side of Jack's face and leaned against his other crutch, whispering something to her before kissing her softly. As they parted, a surprised yet pleased expression remained on Jack's face. She tapped her palm against Scott's chest and whispered something back before pushing away.

Fox tossed her the keys to the truck, and she caught them. "You ready?"

Fox exchanged a knowing smile and nodded. "Thanks again, Scott."

He waved to Fox as they climbed into the truck.

Jack turned the key in the ignition as Fox slammed her door shut. The rock station played another classic they both knew. They put on their sunglasses, rolled down their windows, and waved to Scott, Costa, and Ryan.

They were survivors.

With the addition of Kerry, they were the friends that made it. By chance, or luck, or grace, or sacrifice, or the will to survive—perhaps a different combination for each. None of them had deserved any of what happened that Halloween night, but the ones that died—Elisha, and Luke, and Kennedy, and even Cooper—were only killed because they'd been obstacles to get to *her*.

Fox's chest constricted, and she struggled to breathe with the intrusive thought lingering as usual. Jack reversed down the driveway. As they pulled out, Fox gripped her seatbelt across her chest with both hands, pulling it away, giving herself space to take a full breath.

"You okay?" Jack asked.

Fox gave a small nod, but behind her sunglasses, tears clouded her vision. They drove down the back road toward the center of town, and Fox focused on her breathing.

John Castle was responsible. He was the one who took those lives.

Deep breath in.

She'd killed him so they could escape. She'd done everything she could to protect the people she cared about.

Deep breath out.

She had to keep reminding herself of those facts that she seemed to lose sight of during random times of the day. It wasn't easy to wear those new pathways in her mind when she thought about Luke's wife, and how hard he worked to provide for the future life they dreamt of together, and the hell and heartbreak she must have been going through without him. Or when she'd revisit the day of November first, when their parents and loved ones all learned of the deaths. She wondered if Elisha's parents had to identify her body, and if so, which parts? And Kennedy's sister—her best friend—was the only person who came to deal with the aftermath after losing her. Even Cooper hadn't deserved what happened, and reconciling with whether she could have done more to stop him from coming—stop anyone from dying—took up more of her daily thoughts than anything else.

And that was his purpose.

John had said he'd make Slate, and the mayor, and Fox pay the toll twice for what they'd done, like the Crescent Moon brothers. But he'd been wrong.

She suffered with the burden of all the deaths he caused on his path to get to her that Halloween night. They'd all lost so much, but she still had Jack, and because of her, she could go on. They could go on together—a gift she'd never take for granted again.

As they passed the black, metal picket fence of the cemetery, Fox took her sunglasses off. She squinted at the old maple tree that marked the spot just beside her father's grave. Somehow, the further they drove from him, his presence remained as steadfast as it had since the night she'd quoted him, when his strength, support, and power returned to help her survive and evade death.

She turned to Jack as they stopped before the red traffic light in the intersection. Jack pulled her sunglasses off and reached over to Fox, squeezing her arm, her fingers covering part of the pink scar that ran along it from The Skull's blade. Jack had one of her own on her neck. Time might heal some physical wounds, but not as well as if you took care of them, and more than anything, she was ready for them to take care of each other.

"I'm going to miss it—all of what we had." Fox's voice shook, and she took a deep breath as the tears streamed down her cheeks. "It still feels like home, you know?"

"I miss it, too." Jack took a deep, empathetic breath with her. "And I think it always will."

Fox nodded. "But if I stay, it'll be like living in a cemetery of everything I've lost. Everything's here, and yet everything's gone. Explain that paradox to me."

"There's so much ahead of us. You know that, right?" The light turned green, and with Jack's hand still grasping her arm, she whispered, "Don't look back."

Jack pressed her foot on the gas, and Fox kept her focus on the road ahead.

EPILOGUE

A misty cloud of his breath escaped his lips into the black night above, vanishing before his eyes as he descended the ditch. It wasn't hard to find the tree. The lighter markings left by the car on that fateful Halloween night as it crashed into the maple stood out in contrast against the dull, rough bark, even one year later.

He slipped off his black glove and ran his fingers over the deep gouges and jagged cuts carved into the tree, made just prior to Victoria Castle's body crashing through the windshield, into the clearing below. He squeezed his eyes shut, his abdomen tense as he conjured the image of the scene in his imagination.

When he opened his eyes, he discovered he'd dug his fingernails into a crevice, blood beading by one of his nail beds.

Nature hadn't forgotten the damage done that night, and neither would he.

His black boots shuffled against the bumpy earth as he descended the rest of the hill. Finding flat, solid ground along the same path he'd imagined Victoria's body had flown, he pulled his glove back on, stopping just before the clearing below. He produced the skull mask from where he'd kept it folded in his back pocket, the blood of John's victims still splattered across it. As he pulled it on, a chill crept down his spine, and he clenched his jaw.

Looking out from behind the eyes of the mask that started it all, he pictured John and Victoria's last moments together in that clearing.

For all he knew, they might have lasted minutes, or it could have been hours before the police and paramedics arrived. He doubted he'd ever know the whole truth of what happened after that night, and he wasn't sure he needed to.

A single thought crept into the forefront of his mind as he took one last look at the scene of the event that started it all.

It wasn't finished—not even close.

Thank you for reading **Bleed**, Book #1 in The Skull Serial Killer Thriller Series by bestselling author, Emerald O'Brien.
You can now order Book #2, releasing November 30th, 2023.

Ready for another thriller by Emerald O'Brien?

· · ·

I Heard You Scream

Five can keep a secret if four are dead.

Knock Three Times

Some mistakes haunt your dreams. Others knock at your door.

We Don't Leave

Who can you trust when you can't believe your own eyes?

The Waking Place

Givers must set limits, for takers have none.

Follow Her Home

She's desperate to leave the past behind her. But fear has a way of following.

What She Found

It was supposed to be the perfect getaway, but a knock at the door could ruin their lives.

A knock at the door could ruin their lives.

Givers must set limits, for takers have none.

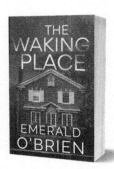

She can't trust her husband. She can't trust herself.

She's desperate to leave the past behind but fear has a way of following.

ALSO BY EMERALD O'BRIEN

Don't miss these suspenseful and unpredictable reads by Emerald O'Brien

Standalone Novels:

Knock Three Times

I Heard You Scream

We Don't Leave

Follow Her Home

The Waking Place

What She Found

The Knox and Sheppard 5 Book Mystery Series:

The Girls Across the Bay (Book One)

Wrong Angle (Book One Point Five, free in Emerald's newsletter)

The Secrets They Keep (Book Two)

The Lies You Told (Book Three)

The One Who Watches (Book Four)

The Sisters of Tall Pines (Book Five)

The Locke Industries Series:

The Assistant's Secret

The Nanny's Secret by best-selling author, Kiersten Modglin

YOUR FREE BOOK

Emerald would love to offer you a free ebook along with updates on her new releases.

Subscribe to her newsletter today on emeraldo-brien.com

ACKNOWLEDGMENTS

Thank you to my first reader, and best friend, Kiersten Modglin. Your encouragement on this one made all the difference. Your enthusiasm lit exactly the fire I needed to bring the story in my heart and mind to life on the page. Thank you for reflecting the story back to me with fresh eyes. I'm so grateful to have your friendship through all the highs and lows of life. Same moon. Love you.

To my sister, Shyla, thank you for being my person, and for not only reading, but helping me with every single book I've ever published. I appreciate you more than I could express, and love you more than you could ever know.

To Sarah at Three Owls Editing, thank you for your professional editing services and insightful feedback. I'm so grateful for your help.

Thank you to my colleagues in the book community for your support, encouragement, and sharing your knowledge with me. I'm proud to call you my friends.

To Sara, I'm so grateful to you for inviting me to the best book club I've had the pleasure of being part of. Thank you, both Erins, June, Heather, and Dee for all the laughs, and all your support.

For the continued support of my family and friends, I

am forever grateful, and I love you all. Each and every person in my life who has supported me and my writing career hold a special place in my heart.

And to my true-blue readers, review team, and newsletter subscribers, I have to thank you for making my dreams come true. Your company on this journey has been a pleasure, and as always, I look forward to meeting you on the next page.

Finally, a special thank you to the creative contributors of the slasher genre. The inspiration for this new series has come in no small part from the decades of thrilling stories I've enjoyed. My hope is to give my readers some of what this genre has given me, including subverted expectations, a thrill ride while you root for the characters you love, and a way to explore the thoughts of confronting some of our worst fears, and facing them together as an audience who can discuss and connect afterwards. I fell in love with the genre for these reasons, but it all began because I took a chance on something new and a little scary. Thank you for taking a chance on my story.

ABOUT THE AUTHOR

Emerald O'Brien was born and raised just east of Toronto, Ontario. She graduated from her Television Broadcasting and Communications Media program at Mohawk College in Hamilton, Ontario.

As a bestselling author of unpredictable stories packed with suspense, Emerald hopes to give her readers some of what her favourite stories have given her, including subverted expectations, a thrill ride while you root for the characters you love, and a way to explore the thoughts of confronting some of our worst fears, and facing them together as an audience who can discuss and connect afterwards.

To find out more, visit Emerald on her website: emeraldobrien.com

If you enjoyed Emerald's work, please share your experience by leaving a review where you purchased the story.

Subscribe to her newsletter for a free ebook, exclusive content, and information about current and upcoming works.